Maximum Trouble

Maximum Trouble

L.M. Pampuro

Maximum Trouble
Copyright 2018 by L.M. Pampuro

This book is a work of fiction.
Names, characters, locations, and events are either a product of the author's imagination, fictitious or used fictitiously.
Any resemblance to any event, locale or person, living or dead, is purely coincidental.

All rights reserved. No part of this book may be used or reproduced by any means, graphic, electronic, or mechanical, including photocopying, recording, taping, or by any information storage retrieval system without written permission of the publisher except in the case of brief quotations embodied in critical articles and reviews.

Cover design by the LMPatarini group

ISBN: 978-1-5323-9569-7

L.M. Pampuro

Maximum Trouble

L.M. Pampuro

This book is gratefully dedicated to my mother, my godfather, and those who continue to inspire me.

Maximum Trouble

L.M. Pampuro

Maximum Trouble

Moist droplets of fluid compressed along Zack Brady's hairline as the vibration of his work boots clamor against the metal stairs within the tight, dank space. He moved with purpose towards the lit exit sign. With force, he opened the door. Bright sunlight reflected up across the colossal pavement. The heat hit his body with full force.

Zack put on his aviators and waited a minute for his eyes to focus. To his right, a massive military jet saddled up to the hanger he exited. On his left, a field bordered by electric fencing. Totally exposed, his destination lay in front. The two-story brick building with a metal connector to another hanger. No planes visibly attached. All doors and windows shut tight.

He sucked in a deep breath. On the exhale, all his attention focused on the path he considered necessary to take. With shoulders back and head held high, he started to walk in the direction of his objective.

"Excuse me, sir," Zack swore under his breath, "May I see your—" He turned in the direction of the young Military Police Officer. The MP's eyes move up and down his dated uniform. Zack waited. The M.P. raised his hand to a salute, "I'm sorry, sir, please continue."

Zack dismissed him with a quick salute. Without a word, he resumed his trek. He turned back to catch the young soldier speaking into his radio. From memory, his strides lengthened as his pace quickened.

He hesitated a breath before opening the windowless metal door. Cold air refreshed his wet face. Bumps developed on his neck with a chill replacing the heat within his body. He allowed his thoughts to drift to Maxi and her family. Once again, he needed to get her out of a jam.

He did a quick scan of the room as Maxi's smile entered his brain. The dentist's office furniture arranged around the perimeter broke only to reveal a door with a phone. He crossed the room in two strides to pick up the receiver. A woman's voice garbled through the handset.

"State your business," she barked.

"I need to see the Admiral now."

His request returned with silence.

Zack waited as the shadows moved behind a large mirror on the wall adjacent to the door. His heartbeat increased. He turned back to the door outside. He silently counted the seconds. One glance went to his wrist armor C28 ``to note the actual time.

Knowledge gave him three minutes. The experience brought the number to two. Another shadow joined the group. Brady had been on the opposite side of the mirror many times. On the other side, this group held a debate about what to do next. His situation could only go in two directions; he either meets with the admiral or is under arrest. He couldn't see the man, yet he knew the M.P. he met crossing the tarmac stood on the opposing side of his escape.

Both scenarios possessed the same level of pressure. He had been thrown in the brig before and hadn't much liked it. Zack needed to move. He paced out ten strides from corner to corner within the confine of the room. He started on a diagonal, changed to walk the parameter, all the while exercising the same step count. Zack inhaled and exhaled to the rhythm of his steps. His arms tucked against his body, although at each corner, he wiggled the fingers on each hand.

He observed more shadows in the mirror. Now an outline he recognized. Broad shoulders, thick torso, with a slim pointed device coming off the right side. "Crap," he muttered aloud.

His body involuntarily let out a jump at the door buzzer. He entered to expectations. Military Police flanked both sides of an older, attractive female. She stood with a well-practiced look of neutrality on her face. Zack folded his hands in plain view. He stood military at ease to wait for her to speak first, not wanting to give anything away.

A military police officer moved behind him to block the exit. The other stayed at attention next to the female, hand resting on his sidearm.

"We've been waiting for you, Mr. Brady," the woman said, without further explanation, adding, "Boys, please escort our friend to the Admiral's conference room." The two men moved to either side of Zack. "Oh, and make certain he is relieved of his weapon before entering the secured area."

Zack felt a hand slipped down his back as the pressure from his firearm disappeared. They patted him down the sides to remove another gun and the knife from his boot. One of the M.P.'s commented, "Nice," as the other displayed the weapon. The mystery woman left through an inconspicuous door on the left. "This way please," one M.P. pointed towards the more prominent door. In the mirrored reflection, the officer stood behind him, his weapon by his side. He acknowledged the directive with a nod to proceed.

"Today must be your lucky day," one of the M.P.'s said.

"I hope so," Zack replied. "I sure hope so."

Maximum Trouble

"Hey, where did the boat come from?" When no one answered, she got more specific, "What kind of boat is the gray one out there?" Maxi pointed her newly French manicured finger out across the Caribbean water. She took a moment to admire how the white tip glistened against the turquoise blue water. Earlier in the morning, she spent an hour at the rooftop spa at the resort where she stayed with her son Ric and parents Rich and Ev. During her manicure, she overlooked the bay. The technician insisted the blue on her nails match the turquoise of the Caribbean Sea. Maxi sat in a pillowed lounge chair to watch the cruise ships dock downtown. She got primped and pampered while the ships did the same to unload their passengers for a fun day on the island.

She arrived on the beach to meet her dad and the group of retirees he hung out with while on the island. Centered in the bay sat a gray metal Unitarian ship that arrived between her

leaving the spa and walking here. The bright, large, luxurious cruise ship pulling out of port behind it gave the boat an appearance of a slightly smaller, yet more hardened vessel.
"It's Navy," said Sam from Long Island. Sam retired from the New York City police department five years ago. And one of the many people Maxi's parents befriended since they started spending the month of February on Aruba years prior. Sam, like most of the group, spent his days sitting under a Divi-divi tree on the beach, watching the world go by in between naps and swims. "I don't recognize if it's ours, though," he frowned. "Rich, take a look and tell me what you think?"
Sam handed his binoculars over to Maxi's dad, who sat on one lounge chair over.
"Naw, the ship's not ours," Rich kept his focus on the boat. "Though the flag looks familiar." Rich handed the binoculars back to Sam. He continued to watch the ship. "Venezuela wants the island back. Maybe the ship belongs to them."
 The group laughed. The big news this year Venezuela decided the Dutch acquired the ABC islands, which consisted of Aruba, Bonaire, and Caracas, illegally, and the islands still belong to Venezuela, not Holland. Daily reports of Chavez made plans to take back what belongs to his country ran on the

news.

"I forgot about Venezuela," Sam said. "I guess Chavez needs a vacation spot." The quip got a laugh from the group.

"Either way, it makes no sense. Seriously, why would any military ships be in the waters off Aruba?" Maxi asked. This was her first real vacation since the fiasco with her ex-husband Jon. Her parents decided to fly Maxi and her son Ric down to Aruba to join them for the last week of their vacation. They figured their daughter needed a break from life, and it would be entertaining to have her and the grandson along.

It took over a year for Maxi to settle the estate since the murder of her ex predated divorce proceedings, none of her paperwork ever got filed. First came the investigation, where she needed to be cleared of murder. Once the evidence proved she didn't contract for Jon to be killed, the trials were scheduled for all the parties involved.

After all, got settled, the famous Gert Fontaine extortion trial began. Maxi played a crucial role in her prosecution. Her mother, as usual, thought Maxi trusted the wrong people. "Maxi should know better," became her new mantra. Maxi's head hurt from her eye-rolling each time her mother pointed this out to anyone who would listen.

There still is, as her parent's hope, the Zack

Brady situation. Her parents wanted to see her married again, even though she and Ric had a good life on their own. Maxi shivered as Zack's face popped up.

They dated on and off before, during, and a little after the trial. He stayed close, yet something was off. Maxi wondered if genuine feelings for her existed or he needed to protect his star witness. Their dates consisted of lunches in between sessions with the lawyers, to prepare Maxi for the defendant's actions. They even told her how to answer their questions.

Maxi's hand rubbed against her lower lip. "Maxi," her dad shrugged his shoulders and reached for a cigarette. "You spend far too much time thinking about stuff that just is." Maxi shrugged in his direction. She walked down towards the water. The hot, white sand slightly burned her raw feet. She should have gone for the pedicure too. Watching the waves let her mind wander. If the sweet ocean smell, the sun reflecting off the water, and occasional hot bodies couldn't take her to another place, she didn't see what could. "I need a distraction," she said aloud. She stood at the water's edge and let the waves roll over her chipping purple toes. The ship now turned sideways, and although the flag appeared more evident, she didn't have a clue about which country it belonged too. "Another mystery," she said aloud.

Maxi walked towards downtown, the turquoise surf splashed as she moved. Along the shore sat parents surrounded by young children building castles. Teenagers played volleyball or lay in the sun moving their heads to the beat only they could hear. Couples held hands and walked gazing into each other's eyes. Every once an in, while someone would remind her of Zack, from the older male, sported six-pack abs in jean shorts to a five o'clock shadow on an angular face, parts of him seemed to always surround her.

"Oh puke," Maxi said aloud as she passed a couple intertwined, lips passionately locked together, standing by the water. She debated for months about asking Zack to join her. As the trial progressed, she became less enchanted with the idea to decide a family vacation with her, and Ric would be better.

They needed a break.

Ric fared much better meeting new people. He found a few kids to hang out with by the pool during the day. He met up with them again to play video games in the resort arcade at night. Ric also indulged himself in other resort activities like beach volleyball and bingo with his grandma. Maxi hesitated on letting him go out at night alone until her mother reminded her he's twelve now and starting to grow up.

"You got to cut them loose sometimes."
Another eye-roll moment.
When Maxi was a teenager, her parents gave her a lot of freedom. She was allowed to go out with friends during the week and stay out to eleven on weekends. Back then, the rules were simple. Keep your grades up. Stay out of trouble, or as Maxi interpreted it, don't get caught.
And most importantly, be responsible. Remembering her old wild streak made Maxi nervous with Ric. *If he does half the things I did,* ...she'd say to her mother, and her mother's response was always "Ya and look how bad you turned out."
Maybe she did need to allow him to make his own mistakes.
It must be her imagination taking over because the mystery ship appeared to move closer to shore. She stared at the strange markings on the side. "Definitely not ours," she said to herself.
She continued to walk past the Jet Ski rentals, banana boat rides, the topless sunbathers, finally arriving at the Marquee Resort. Maxi cut up across the beach and walked into the pool area eyes straight ahead, focused on the giant terra cotta water cooler. She reached over, selected a paper cup, and filled it like a guest of the resort. She had

strolled with her mother earlier, who shocked her with the same process. *What are they going to do, check my bathing suit?* Ev said while laughing. *Its only water, Maxi.*

"The boat out there's Afghanistan," she overheard someone say.

"Didn't realize they had a Navy," another answered.

"Me neither. It makes you wonder where our boys are." She couldn't see either man speaking but noted the one who identified where the boat was from had a slight English accent.

"Probably in the Persian Gulf, wouldn't you say?" The other gentlemen didn't respond.

Maxi chugged her water, threw the cup in the barrel, and headed back to the beach. Her eyes drifted to the gray boat, each time appearing closer. Maxi noted the ship itself, minus the markings, could easily be mistaken for a United States naval vessel. Both had the same dull gray color, the same intimidating steel design, and as the memory of visiting her brother, Commander Pete Malone, at one of his many stations came flooding back, the same forbidding presence.

"Out there is not a friendly boat," she noted as her pace quickened.

The retirees were still sitting under the tree. Sam had fallen asleep. The Italians were speaking amongst themselves while Rich and another guy, some stockbroker from Philly, chatted about pension plans.

"Some guy at the Marquee said the ship was Afghanistan," Maxi said to no one in particular.

"Maxi, your imagination works overtime," Rich said. He went back to the view of the bay.

"Your mother is at Bingo by the pool. I think Ric is with her." That was her clue to skedaddle. Maxi picked up her towel.

"I guess I'll join her," she answered. When no one asked her to stay, she headed towards the crosswalk connected the resort to the beach.

The pool area consists of three bodies of water connected by a waterfall and several bridges. Blue umbrellas and lounge chairs surround each section along with small grass huts housing towel distribution, soft drinks, and snacks. Over closer to the main building, in a shady area, sits a kiddy pool with a small slide.

The bar is housed in a large grass hut open on three sides directly in front of the biggest pool. The bar faced the most giant waterslide, tucked in between rocks and palm trees. The screams echo through the courtyard as each slider took their turn. The higher the pitch, the more Maxi cringed. It was the squeal of a little girl. Little girls possess the most annoying screams, Maxi noted. "Boys don't scream," Ric reminded her all the time. "Boys aren't wimps."

She walked around the side of the bar, hearing B-9 being said over the speaker. "Late again," she groaned.

Her mom sat in front of the caller, to the slight left of the bar. On the chair next to her, sat Ric. He helped his grandmother coordinate the four cards arranged within view across the table in front.

Ric saw Maxi and shouted, "Over here, mom," adding, "You missed the first game."

"Oops," Maxi said, adding a grin. "I walked down to the Marquee, and I guess it took longer than I expected." Ric handed Maxi one of his cards and moved over in his chair, giving her enough room to sit.

"We are doing a square in the middle now," he explained. Ev, Maxi's mom watched over at the two and smiled.

"Pay attention," she scolded. "They called N-32 and G-59."

Ric slid the red cover over the two numbers.

"B-10, B-10," the caller droned.

"NO B's," Ric and Ev yelled back in unison. They looked at each other and began to laugh.

"You are creating a monster," Maxi said.

"N-37, N three seven," the drone continued.

"BINGO!" Someone shouted from the back of the bar. A cute little curly-haired girl about eight in a pink flowered bikini proudly walked

over to where the caller sat in the shade.
"Well, that went well," Ev noted. "I'll tell you, we can't pick cards to save our lives."
"Grandma, I did my best," Ric said.
"I see you did, sweetheart," Ev fluffed her grandson's hair. "You are a good boy." Ric lit up with his grandma's compliment. "So, Max, your father still holding court?" Holding court is what her mom referred to when her dad and the retirees started to debate something. "Your dad can talk and talk and talk...."
"He's on the beach, probably napping by now." The comment got a smile from her mom. One slept on the beach while the other went back to the room for a break. At least they still coordinated for dinner.
"Next game is four corners and a full card," the drone went on. "Four corners will pay twenty dollars while the full card will pay a hundred dollars and a La Cabana t-shirt." A deep, almost wheezy sounding, inhale resonates over the speaker, "The first number is B-4. B-4."
"You know, mom, if they had games for longer than an hour, this guy would put everyone asleep."
"I-22. I-22."
"You got that right," Ev said as she slid the red cover over I-22.
"There's a weird boat out in the bay," Maxi

started to explain.

"Yeah, we saw it this morning while you two slept." Ev got aggravated; her daughter and grandson were sleepers. "They're wasting the best part of the day," could be heard more than once this week through the rooms' thin walls. Both Maxi and Ric responded with a simple move to put the pillows over their ears, before melting back to dreamland.

"I heard it's from Afghanistan," Maxi said casually.

"Afghanistan? Where on earth did you hear this?" One of the Italian women interrupted. "Why would they need boats? They live in the desert."

"From a guy at the Marquee."

"The Marquee," the Italian women said back repulsed. "Figures."

"I'm sure it's not from anywhere dangerous, Maxi," her mom said. "If it was, Pete would call to tell us to leave."

Maxi nodded her head and leaned back in the wicker chair. This forced Ric to sit forward. Here they were thousands of miles away, and as always, Pete was with them. If not physically, spiritually since he was the chosen child. At times, Maxi thought her parents blamed her messy divorce on her lack of judgment versus the professional con artist who took advantage of a bad situation. After all, this would never happen to Pete. Pete's wife was perfect, if not slightly psychotic. She had to admit he and the wife produced two fabulous kids. Both excelled in what they do. There are times she wonders if her mother could be right.

The boat in the bay bothered her enough to consider calling Zack, or she needed an excuse to hear his voice. When he drove Ric and her to the airport, Zack seemed preoccupied, a constant state of being for him Maxi discovered over the last months. When he was on a case, he micro-focused on his case. So even on off days, work still occupied his thoughts. His speech would wander off in the middle of a conversation to make a note of something that had popped into his head, so he could remember later. Of course, none of the revelations could be shared. Zack labeled it all as confidential.

"You understand, don't you, Max?" he'd say. She wanted to scream, "No, I don't!" yet the voice in her head stopped her with a simple "why bother."

Zack started to distance himself as the O'Hara trial progressed. Maxi figured it was a matter of time before he left her. She waited so long to date Zack Brady she wasn't going to make ending it easy on him to dump her. If she had thought it through, she probably would have dropped him early on, if only to save herself

another heartbreak. That was Maxi, according to her mom, never thinking things through. Maybe she should send him a quick email. Something nonchalant like *hi, how are you, hear of any Afghanistan boats in the Caribbean?* She started to laugh. She shook her head from side to side. Maxi focused in time to catch Ric and her mother's gaze, one of concern, the other wide-eyed.
"B-6 is not funny, mom," Ric lectured like a teacher in training.
Her mom watched not saying a word.
"I just had a hilarious thought," Maxi said. She turned towards her mom, adding, "It was warped. You wouldn't appreciate it." Ev nodded in agreement as she continued to cover her bingo card.
"I think I'm going to check my email after this," Maxi rearranged the cards in front of her. "In case anything important came up."

Spencer Cabot slammed the phone into the receiver. His assistant jumped from her desk. Their two bodies met as he pushed passed her in the doorway.

"Mister," she started to say yet stopped as he raised his hand in the air. She watched her boss bang his finger into the call button for the elevator. He paced as he waited. At her count of ten, he turned in the direction of the stairs.

The door to the stairwell closed at the same time the elevator arrived.

Spencer took the stairs two at a time. He pushed open the stairwell door, almost hitting one of the building delivery people.

"Hey," the kid yelled. Spencer scowled back at the kid as he moved in the opposite direction. He arrived at the office in the back to find Marjorie filing her nails at her desk.

"Hey, Spence," she greeted him. She threw the file in her top drawer. "What's up?"

"Where's your boss?" he bellowed as he peered into the empty office.

"Don't have a clue. He wasn't here when I came in."

Spencer took a long inhale. Marjorie appeared as a decoration behind the desk, yet sometimes he wondered about her mental capacity. "Wait, he didn't come in today?"

"No. I opened the office up and haven't seen him since yesterday." Spencer winced. His hand rubbed the back of his neck. "Did I miss something?"

"I got a call from someone in D.C. requesting Mr. Brady for assignment." Spencer waited. "Please tell me you have some knowledge of what this is, Marjorie?"

"No clue. Seriously, Spence, you are paranoid. I told you yesterday about the website he visited. Didn't you check the links?" Spencer nodded. "So, he was following something online. I swear since he got back the other day from bringing that woman to the airport..."

Spencer walked into Zack's office. The desk contained a few scattered papers, along with a pile of unopened mail. He walked around to the opposite side. Marjorie had moved to sit on the small couch in the corner.

"Something is missing," Spencer said. This brought Marjorie closer. Both stared at the desk.

"The photo," Marjorie pointed to an empty

spot. "The one with the kid."
"Zack doesn't have any kids."
"Are you kidding me? He does. Two with the ex," Marjorie said. "But that isn't the photo I was talking about."
"He has kids? I never knew." Spencer shrugged. "So whose kids are in the missing photo?"
"Not his!" Marjorie stared behind Spencer. He turned in the direction of her focus.
"What!" he shouted.
"Maxi, that's her name. The one from the trial. Her photo was here," she pointed to the same spot as before. "Did he put it in his desk?"
Spencer sat in Zack's high back chair. He opened the top drawer. Pens, pencils, empty note pads. The top side drawer held the same. He pulled on the middle drawer. Stuck. The bottom one contained files.
He fingered each, yet they appeared to be the same cases assigned from the start. "Marjorie, I need you to go through these files. Look for update notes." She nodded. "And figure out this drawer." He pulled on the middle one again.
"Did you ever think it's locked? Did he leave the key?"
Spencer stared back at Marjorie. "No, he didn't leave a key," he retorted. "Marjorie, I don't like this. First, he's in a restricted area

on the computer, now the boy disappeared. I think we need to file some sort of paperwork."
"What about—"
"Let's not worry for now. We can't have Mr. Brady running around unsupervised, can we?"
"Got it, boss." Marjorie gave a little salute. "Shall we terminate him?" she giggled.
"No. No, let's 4271 him. He'll be locked out of everywhere." He watched Marjorie's eyes sparkle. "And babe, get this freakin' drawer open," he started to leave before adding, "please," at the end.

"**M**r. Brady, how splendid of you to join us," Admiral Edels greeted from the opposite end. Zack could identify most of the people in the room from previous work along with reputation. His stance relaxed a bit upon seeing Pete, Maxi's brother, sitting to the right of the admiral. While others sat at attention, on the other side of the table Donald Atwood, his former squad commander, stretched his legs out.

Zack gave a courtesy nod and waited. "Please have a seat," The Admiral signaled to chair at the opposite end. Zack noted both Military Police stood at attention to block the exit. "For those who do not know, this is Zack Brady, one of our finest officers—"

"Who makes stupid decisions," Pete blurted out. "Did you really walk out of New Haven?" Zack nodded. "What were you thinking?"

"I was thinking an old friend needed my help," Zack answered. He sat tall in the chair. When he locked eyes with Pete, Zack's jaw started to make a twitching motion. He heard his heartbeat increased with each silent second.

"Okay, boys, calm down," Admiral Edels turned his concentration onto Zack. "We appreciate your assistance, and are going to take advantage of your skillset, however," he turned towards Atwood, "Do you want to tell him or should I?" Atwood gave a slight shrug in return. Edels continued, "Zack, there is a slight problem. It will take me at least three weeks to obtain your security clearances back, and frankly, we don't have the time."

"Get my clearances back? I should still have full authorization."

"Yeah – dipshit. When you quit all your security clearances were revoked," Pete replied.

"Pete, I never quit. I didn't show up for work."

"Walked out on the FBI, at least that is the story we are getting," Pete interjected. "Your idiot boss pulled all your clearances even though he knew you were coming down here to assist in the current situation."

"How did he find out?" Zack's right leg began to bounce, an old habit from grade school that started when he got extremely agitated. Working in government, he had come up with more discrete movements, yet today he had a skewed sense of balance. When no one spoke, Zack repeated, "Would someone please tell me how Spencer Cabot knew what I planned to do?"

Pete let out a massive whoosh of air. "I tried to follow the procedure and ask permission for you to temporarily join our team. Your supervisor said no, your portion of The Shadow investigation wasn't complete, and he couldn't reassign it."

"That's bullshit."

"I know – but in the following procedure when you, my hot-headed friend, didn't show up for work today, he pulled all clearances even though he knew you were most likely heading here."

"So, I'm out?"

"Not at all, Mr. Brady," Admiral Edels jumped back in. "We found a way around most of the hurdles. The rest we'll work on. As of today, you are part of our team as a government contractor."

"What does a contractor mean exactly?"

"It means you are part of the mission to save Americans, including the Captain's family, yet you do not have a top security clearance any longer." Zack brought his hand to his chin to stroke. Pete watched while his fingers punched something into his phone. "Mr. Brady?"

"Yes, Admiral. I am considering this approach and want to make certain I understand what is expected of me."

"You'll go on the drop," Pete started to explain, "yet your goal will be to move Americans and others if necessary, to safety. The tactile team, who will travel with you, will go after the people responsible."

"Will I have a firearm?"

"Yes."

"Will I have back up?"

"Yes."

"Is my primary mission to find Pete's family?"

"Off the record – yes, and a few others. We will explain later on." Admiral Atwood said before Pete could speak.

"Thank you," Pete muttered.

"I'm in."

"Splendid. Pete, take Zack to reinstate his papers and such and then conduct the briefing with the team. Let's say at four."

"Yes, sir," Pete stood and saluted. He gave a head nod to Zack, who stood and repeated the action.

"Thank you," Zack said as he vanished through the door.

The Admiral sat back in his chair, "Do you really think this is the best idea?"

"I know Zack Brady. He can handle this assignment. But one small thing is nagging me."

"Probably the same thing that is bugging me—"

"Spencer?"

"Correct. What is his motive for being a prick?"

"Exactly what I was thinking. At one point, Zack had mentioned Spencer had a micromanagement approach that made it difficult for him to accomplish his job."

"Do you think he missed the action?

"Maybe. Though I believe there is more to the Spencer situation."

"So, do I."

Maximum Trouble

Maxi headed up to the business center after the rousing game of bingo. Her mom had waited twice with the same number, N-37. As if the bingo Gods were testing them, Ric waited on the last game for N-37 for one hundred dollars and a t-shirt, which he generously offered to give to Maxi.

"Mom, it's because I love you," he said with a grin as a little old lady yelled, "bingo!"

The business center was a loose term for the area to the left of a bar situated upstairs from the lobby. Here eight desks were arranged in rows. Each desk contained two computers. To use, one only had to buy an access code from the front desk. At twenty American dollars an hour, with most of the machines always in use, some island entrepreneurs did reasonably well.

At least Maxi hoped it was a native. At too many of these tourist destinations, the natives get screwed out of making a living by some greedy outsider. Living full-time in a tourist

area, she knew this from experience.
Maxi sat at the same computer every day, the furthest from the bar, with back up against a wall. Although there were cameras everywhere, here she had the illusion of a little privacy.
She hit the space bar and proceeded to enter her access code. Maxi tried to check emails once a day to make sure what was left of her company hadn't gone under while she disappeared for a week. Her assistant, Nancy, took charge. Maxi knew the situation was in capable hands. Yet, her name still appeared on the shutter. As part of her personality, she needed to feel in control, especially after her recent stretch of not having any.
The screen lit up, and she proceeded to her email portal. After typing in her access code, Maxi was surprised to see she had zero new messages. Nancy must be checking too.
"Well, this sucks," she said aloud. She hit new and began typing. *There's a weird-looking ship off the coast of the island. I may be paranoid, yet I figured you'd know and call up and say I'm crazy. Let me know. Love Max.* She typed in the first few letters of her brother's email, hit send, sat and debated about sending Zack a quick note.
I should touch base to make sure... Her thought trailed off as a very tan dread locked

gentleman in a loud Hawaiian shirt, and red Bermuda shorts sat down at the computer next to her. He gave Maxi a quick smile as he started to type in an access code.

Maxi logged out of email and switched over to a local news website to see what else she was missing. While the page loaded, her stomach flipped. A glance towards the bar caught one of the men watching her. Promptly, she clicked on the box to log off. Her screen went blank. Maxi got up and walked around the stranger to leave. She noted all the other computers on the floor were empty. A few men sat at the bar dressed similar to the guy who had sat down next to her. At this time of day, the upstairs bar had no one to serve drinks.

Maxi walked quickly by, feeling their eyes follow her down the stairs. About halfway down, she heard someone say, "Tourist. No big deal," in a heavy Spanish accent. She waited to hit the bottom of the stairs before reaching for her cell.

"Hey Pete, its Max. Listen, my gut is telling me something weird is happening here. Any reason to worry?" Without delay, she pressed send for Zack's number. As it began to ring, she clicked off, put her phone back in her pocket, to wait with irritation for a response from her brother.

Rich and Ev made reservations at their favorite restaurant, Madame Jeannette's, months in advance of their trip. They up'd their reservation to four to make sure Maxi and Ric got the full island experience. This was their third visit during this stay. The host greeted them like old friends.

"Richie, Evy, you come back, and who do you bring with you?" He bellowed as the group walked towards the hostess station. After introductions were made, the host escorted the group through the bar area to the back of the restaurant. The outside terrace surrounded by lush green gardens appeared busy yet not overcrowded. The greens gave patrons the illusion of privacy while giving staff little inlets to assist in providing patrons their undivided attention.

Once they sat, their waiter brought out a massive plate of the morning made pumpkin, corn, banana, and cinnamon slices of bread coupled with honey-sweetened whipped butter. He read the specials then disappeared, only to return with drinks and tropical salads of lettuce, tomato, papaya, and cucumbers in a mango dressing. He took the dinner requests then, promptly moved out of view.

"I'm so full," Maxi exclaimed as he returned later to clear the salad plates.

"Too bad you need to eat some more," he joked back. Moments later, he balanced several plates piled high with food before them. The smell engulfed the area. Ev and Maxi opting for fresh grilled mahi-mahi caught this morning off the coast. Their plates were covered with cilantro butter sauce, fried plantains, cabbage salad, and rice.

Ric and Rich both had beef. Rich opting for the king's cut prime rib, "I realize I always order the same thing, but I don't want to chance you'll make me something I won't like as much," he said to the table as he ordered.

Ric chose something called a Butcher's Cut. Some sort of roast marinated in bacon fat for three days before slow-cooked to perfection. When his entrée arrived, it was large enough for the whole table. Along with his personal roast beef, he had garlic rice and steamed island vegetables.

After trying a taste, Rich commented he was ordering the entree next time if he remembered the name. Everyone laughed, including the waiter. "That's okay," the waiter smiled, "I'll remember for you."

Ric ate every bite of his entrée, so when the waiter mentioned dessert selections, he stated, "I need to walk a bit before I need a sweet."

"I like this kid!" The waiter exclaimed as he handed the check to Rich. Maxi offered to pay, yet her father's response was always the same. "Get it now or get it later."

As a cluster, they walked along hotel row and the boardwalk. "Hey, we can eat dessert, too," Ric added.

"Sounds good to me," his grandfather replied. Ev and Maxi's hand automatically flew to their stomachs.

"This doesn't seem very crowded," Maxi commented several times.

"Yeah, well, they are all probably gambling already," another standard Rich response.

The moon sparkling over the ocean with the waves softly rolling on to the sand gave a wonderful sense of peace for Maxi. She stared out at the water, every once in a while, giving her mom an "ah huh," although she wasn't listening to a word Ev said.

Instead, Maxi let her mind wander. The the battleship was out of view, and she could see nothing but water, stars, and the moon for miles. The boardwalk creaked at they strolled against their dinner weight, as Ric liked to call it. Her dad was wearing his favorite shirt. On the back, it read, "I'm retired. Go around." On the front, it said, "See the back of the shirt."

People would stroll by commenting on it or laughing after they had passed. The evening took on more of a relaxed pace. Maxi could feel her heartbeat slowing to a tempo she hadn't experienced in years.

After a stop so Rich and Ric could order ice cream, they arrived back to the lobby to find crowds of people screaming at the front desk, suitcases stacked up alongside each group. Rich spotted Sam on the other side of the lobby. The group pushed their way through the crowd to where Sam stood with his wife.

Sam turned as they approached. Rich saw he was on the phone, so he turned to Celia, Sam's wife, "Did we miss something? We just got back from Madame Jeanette's."

"Lucky you," she responded. "Madame Jeanette's is a wonderful last meal." Sam shot Celia a look. Instantly she closed her mouth. He hung up his phone and pulled Rich aside from the group.

"Something is going on. The airports closed. Something about an emergency. They said no planes in or out for at least a week."

"What? Why?"

"Exactly what I was trying to find out. This could be tied into the boat we saw earlier. The hotel left this under our door."

Rich read the notice. *Sorry for the inconvenience*; it read. H*owever, anyone holding an American passport must leave the island immediately. The US Government is sending a cruise ship that will pick up all American visitors at 10 am at the dock downtown. Anyone who chooses to stay on the Island of Aruba does so illegally, at their own risk.*

"The government is sending a cruise ship?" Rich said. "That doesn't sound right." Rich pulled out his cell phone and press autodial. "Hey, sonny boy," he spoke into the receiver. "We were told the government is sending a ship for us to leave Aruba, what is going on? Call back ASAP!" Rich hung up, hit another number, and left the same message again. "Hold tight," he said to Sam. "I called my son. He's in DC. I'll let you know when he calls back." Rich turned to Maxi. "Maxi, maybe you should...."

"I texted him while you were on the phone," Maxi replied.

"Maxi's boyfriend..." Ev started to explain.

"He's not my boyfriend—"

"I thought Zack was your boyfriend, mom?" Ric chimed in.

"It's complicated. Anyway..."

Ev stage whispered to Celia, "Zack works for

the FBI. He was dating Maxi, but now," she shrugged, "Well, if he still was her boyfriend, he might be here…"

"Mom!"

"I suggest we go back to the condo and pack, just in case. Celia and Sam, you are welcome to come with us as I hope to hear something back soon from my boy."

"Thanks, Rich. Celia, you can go. I'm going to wait here to try to obtain more information."

"I'm staying with you," Celia replied as she linked her arm around his.

"You know where we are," Rich added as the group walked away. No one spoke until the door to the condo was shut.

"Richie…" Ev started talking, "This is too weird. We should pack," she began to pull out suitcases from the hallway closet. She covered the bed as she opened both up.

"I'm thinking we wait to hear from Pete. He's our best bet to find out what is going on. The government sending a cruise ship sounds funny. It doesn't feel right."

Maxi put her arm around Ric and hugged him. "It's all going to be okay."

Pete led Zack through a series of unidentified metal doors leading down a long grey hallway. They walked in silence. He entered a room with several metal desks, all manned by a uniform personal. Zack noted three out of five of the desks sported lines of at least a dozen people, some in uniform, most not.

On the far side, Pete led Zack over to a female officer. Her eyes stayed locked on her screen. "Unless you are an officer in any branch of the United States Military, your line is over there," she pointed with one hand. At the same time, she continued to type with the other.

Pete stood silent and waited. He watched her eye continue to move across her computer screen, yet her gaze did not raise to meet his. Zack looked around the room. This was the part of government work he hated. *Just do your job,* he pleaded to the woman, as he observed Pete. He knew what was coming and felt sorry for what the woman would encounter.

Pete cleared his throat, "I need an I.D. for a government contractor to be issued now," he said. His voice calm yet direct.

"Contractors need to fill out an A-14, A-37, B-35, and C-9 along with the standard application. You will find these on the back wall, and the line to procure an I.D. processed, providing the paperwork is in order is over there." Her right hand pointed while her left kept typing.

Pete cleared his throat again, "Sargent Meyers is it?" Hearing her name, she stopped typing. She glanced up at Pete, with one motion, jumped up and saluted before his next words out.

"Yes, sir," she barked. "Name, please?" She turned her full attention to Zack.

"Zack Brady," and to save time, Zack recited his Social Security number before her request. Pete watched Sargent Meyers' brow furor as she typed Zack's information. He caught Zack's eye and tilted his head in her direction. She continued to stare at the screen.

"Huh..."

"Problem?"

With a deep inhale, Sargent Meyers explained, "There is a block on this Social. I can't issue your I.D. You need to—" Pete turned his back, cellphone already in his hand. Zack watched him step away from the desk to walk to an area with fewer people.

"This can't be right," they heard him say as both Zack and the Sargent watched Pete's right hand moving as he spoke into the receiver. They waited.

"This is weird," Sargent Meyer commented.

"What is?"

"The block went away. Okay – let's finish this," Sargent Meyer prompted. "Name, check. Social, check. Permanent address?" Zack observed Pete still in the conversation as he automatically answered each question. When the Sargent reached, "Last employer," Pete reappeared at their side.

"Federal Bureau of Investigation, New Haven," Zack recited. "And before that United States Navy, Special Forces." Sargent, Meyers nodded. She handed Zack five pages from her printer.

"Take this with you to the officer behind me. I assume you can skip the line, too," she smiled at Pete, "They'll direct you to the next step. Please make certain to sign or initial each page. Have a nice day."

"You too. And thank you for your help." Zack walked around the desk and headed towards the next clerk.

Pete waited until he got out of earshot before asking, "Sargent Meyer, what was the code on the block?"

"4271, why?"

"No reason. The faster Mr. Brady receives credentials, the sooner we can take care of a potential situation." The Sargent nodded. He watched Pete move in the direction of the processing center.

Maxi got little sleep between her phone buzzing and her dad talking in the other room. She wished years earlier, when they had the option to secure Italian dual citizenship, her family had taken advantage of the opportunity. Maxi knew enough Italian to get by, and of course, her parents had learned most the swear words. Ric was the only one who knew a foreign language fluently as he had been taught French since kindergarten. She considered the others in the room. Her family certainly could not pass for French. With their features, they all had more American features than Europeans. When visiting Amsterdam years earlier, a street vendor hassled her as she walked Warmoesstraat Street into the city. Fed up, she stopped to ask how they knew she was an American. She wore the same clothing and hairstyle as everyone else in the area. The man had replied Americans project a certain presence, a smell even, they stand out everywhere they go.

Right now, she wished whatever the presence, it would go away fast.

Sam had stopped by earlier. Rich and he exchanged information in hushed tones. The debate continued about the cruise ship. Pete had said no such agreement had taken place and to sit tight. The hotel put out notice at this time Americans were no longer welcome at the property, and all had to leave. They would provide transportation to the main dock downtown tomorrow morning.

"I think we should go downtown and check out what is happening. Hopefully, we can find answers there," she had heard Sam suggest.

"My son said to sit tight, but if we can't stay here..." Sometime between their exchange and the morning, it was decided the group would head downtown. The meeting time was ten a.m. in the lobby.

Shouts could be heard from the moment they exited the room, and the yelling got louder, the closer the group got to the lobby area.

"What do you mean I can't take a shuttle?" they heard an angry patron shout. "You said the hotel would provide transportation."

They could hear the manager saying, "The shuttles left. You need to use a taxi service or walk." Usually very composed, Maxi watched his eyes switch focus between the mass in his lobby and another distraction over by the stairs. She peeked around the corner. Against the wall, watching the manager, leaned the man who sat next to her yesterday in the business center. Arms crossed in front, his gaze never wavered from the man in the suit. The more he stared, the more sweat appeared on the manager's face.

Maxi moved out of view. "Dad, I think we need to leave now." Rich's eyes widened.

"Really?" sarcasm oozed in his reply.

"There is a man over there who was in the business center at the same time as I was yesterday. He sat too close to me and," her hand flew to her stomach. Rich rolled his eyes yet made a motion towards the back door.

"Let's go out this way and load the suitcases in the car," he said. Maxi followed her parents. Once their four suitcases were arranged, Maxi's carry on and Ric's backpack were squeezed in the back. "We'll go downtown and leave the car on a side street. I'll go check out the situation, and we'll figure out what to do from there."

Sam drove up and pulled his car alongside Rich's sedan. "Ready?" Rich nodded.

Maximum Trouble

Pete caught up with Zack as an officer handed him a lament I.D. "Briefing is now scheduled for nine tomorrow. Do you need anything between now and then? You are welcome to stay at our place tonight."

"Thanks. I will take you up on that if I arrive back from Connecticut at a decent hour. I need my other sidearm," he watched Pete's eyes widen and lowered his voice, "I wasn't sure how this was going to go. I left the office and hopped the Acilla to be here as quick as I could. If you needed me to leave today—"

"You would adapt."

"I would adapt, yet I would rather use equipment I am familiar with."

"I understand. Let me make a call and see if I can get you into Tweed."

"That would be great. I could cab it home and then drive to your place. Probably be back late tonight," he added, "And if you could get back my grandfather's knife..." Pete made a quick note.

"Zack, I want to hear the New Haven story. I'm warning you in advance."

"When I return, we'll talk."

As Zack opened his front door, his phone began to buzz. One glance at the caller I.D. sent his stomach into a frenzy.

"Spencer, what do I owe the pleasure," Zack answered as he lowered his bag off his shoulder.

"So, you clocked out indefinitely?" Zack cringed at the bark.

"I tried to take a day off."

"Zack, don't bullshit me."

"There is a situation—"

"You had a job, and it doesn't include working outside this department!"

"Spencer, my old unit buddy, needs a hand, and I got to go. Your military. You comprehend this." Zack smiled at his slip. While he was off in Afghanistan and other foreign locals working directly for Uncle Sam, good old Spencer hung out in his frat house, drinking beer, and smoking weed.

"It doesn't matter. Zack, we are in the middle of an investigation."

"Spencer, you had me pushing papers. All the evidence you need to move forward is already collected. You could give the project to Marjorie to complete." Zack waited in silence for a response. His attention flipping between the clock on the stove and the conversation.

"Zack, you need to understand—"

"I do, Spencer. I guess I needed to tell you I

quit." Zack disconnected, noting the cellphones did not give the same satisfaction of cradle versions when one aggressively ends a conversation. He went into his bedroom closet, reached up in the back of the top shelf, to pull down a small computer. He went back to his travel bag and placed the second machine alongside his personal laptop. As his phone continued to vibrate, Zack consciously moved objects around the room. When satisfied, he took out his cell, held it up to video. Bit by bit, he moved deliberately around the room.

Upon completion, he took the file and emailed it to himself. Once sent, he clicked on the original and moved the icon to the trash. Promptly emptying the garbage after. He reached into his dresser drawer to pull out a small firearm. He checked the lock, reached for the box of bullets, sitting behind his bible, and threw everything into his bag.

Zack cut his arrival in D.C. short. Traffic along the Jersey Turnpike moved at a snail's tempo due to a construction set up. When he had finally got his speed back, there appeared to be an accident on 95 in Maryland.

He arrived at Pete's house in the Virginia suburbs closer to sunrise than night time. Pete greeted him at the door in sweats and an Old Navy t-shirt.

"'Bout time," Pete commented. Zack noted the

disheveled hair and figured he had slept on the sofa, waiting.

"Love the ole Jersey Turnpike," he stated as Pete offered a Budweiser. "Thanks. After my drive, I needed this."

"And needless to say, I appreciate you helping me out yet—"

"You want to understand why I quit."

"You quit?"

"Yes, about, how many hours did it take to drive back here? It doesn't matter when. Do you really need to know?"

"I do. This can't all be about my sister." Zack's laugh rumbled as Pete immediately shushed him. "Wife and kids," he nodded towards the hallway.

"Sorry. It's just you are aware of how I feel about your sister, yet I would never walk away from my job for her, at least not until I'm in my 50's." Zack sat in a big recliner. "You understand how I have that gut thing?" Pete nodded. "When Spencer Cabot appeared at my office door right after you had me review the map, well, something didn't feel right."

"You quit because your boss made a security inquiry? That doesn't sound like you."

"It was more. Take Marjorie for example—"

"Who is Marjorie?"

"My useless secretary. This woman did absolutely nothing. I mean, she was completely inept, yet when I asked Spencer for a new assistant, he declined."

"What was his reasoning?"

"She's an old friend from Wesleyan," Pete returned an exaggerated eye roll, "Except she didn't graduate, from college, ever."

"Ever?"

"Wesleyan, Brown, Georgetown, University of Southern Florida, you follow the picture?"

"Interesting. No undergrad degree."

"Yeah, very. Bachelors is a job requirement for every position at the agency, even to clean the toilets. You gave me the reason I searched for the past month."

"Well, you are welcome." Pete moved his legs to lie on the couch. "So..."

"So, what is our plan?"

"Have you heard from Maxi?" Zack nodded, no. "I got an email that sounded strange. Military boat off the coast. Weird people, by Maxi's standards, in the public computer area. We both are aware Maxi is more paranoid since the Gert incident yet my gut," Pete patted his stomach, "says otherwise. I also got a call from my parents about some cruise ship the government is sending to move Americans off the island."

"That is very generous, yet I bet our government isn't springing for a ship."

"I told him to stay put, and I'd be in touch in the morning." Zack glance at his phone to see a text from Maxi. He quickly read the contents.

"Actually, I got a communication from Maxi. Basically, the same message you received." Pete nodded.

"It is nice she is keeping you in the loop." Zack laughed aloud. "Hi?" His hand flew over his mouth to mute the sound.

"This shows desperation, at least on your sister's part."

"Or my father asked her to send it." Pete watched Zack's hand move to his stomach. He pointed at the gesture. "Not a good sign, buddy. Not a good sign."

Maximum Trouble

Downtown Oranjastend had more people than usual for a weekday. A long line of busses parked along the prominent boulevard, while an even longer line of tourists wrap around the customs building and slunk down the sidewalk along the festival parade route. Piles of tagged suitcases filled one commercial dock, while another lead to a mega cruise ship bearing no company insignia.

Rich found a parking space on one of the back streets. Only two streets down from the main drag, yet it possessed an uncomfortable silence. The only humans in sight appeared to be the six in front of Rich's car. Sam began, "The long line is to get on the ship. Armed men are walking back along, and the only thing I can see is people are checked as they arrive at the dock. The luggage is on another commercial dock, but I couldn't see a connection."

"You got all that from around the corner?" Maxi inquired.

"We don't fool around in the city," Sam responded. "I say we stick together and head towards the end of the line. There we might get hold of more information and hopefully hear from your kid."

"Didn't Pete say to hang tight?" Ev grabbed Ric's hand. "Now, don't let go of me," she instructed. Ric smiled up at his grandma.

"Yes – unfortunately, we couldn't stay at the hotel," Rich answered.

Sam lead the group while Maxi noted her father hung back. She turned to catch him, checking over his shoulder several times. The empty streets made moving easier, yet at each intersection, they moved faster to cross. As the main drag grew closer, Maxi moved to take Ric's other hand. He smiled up at her.

"Don't worry mom—"

"Are you American?" they stopped at the sound of a booming voice. All turned to see a young man holding a machine gun. He repeated, "Are you American?"

Sam and Rich exchanged glances. Maxi felt a vibration in her purse. Her father's phone rung too because she watched his hand automatically reach for his front shirt pocket. The man raised his gun.

"Yes, we are American," Sam said. His voice level.

The man glanced back over his shoulder. "Oh,

you need to move to the line over there." He pointed towards the sidewalk. Sam nodded as the group moved as one into the direction indicated. The young man, satisfied, disappeared from their view.

"Now, what do we do?" Celia asked. Others were brought in behind them as the line moved foot by foot. All watch another cruise ship dock off the coast, again with no company insignia. As they moved closer to the tourist information building, Rich and Sam nodded towards the men's room.

"Just sit tight," they instructed.

Maxi remembered her phone had buzzed. She dug it out of the bottom of her purse to click on messages. Zack's voice was calm, yet direct, "Maxi, this is Zack. I'm with Pete, and he said to tell you not to board the boat. He called your dad too, but either way, tell your parents, okay. I want you to try to head to the middle of the island and call me as soon as you hear this." The recording stopped.

"Maxi, what's wrong? You are pale as a seashell."

"Mom, that was Zack." The line moved around the corner. Twenty feet or so in front of them, armed soldiers checked papers and passports. "We need to bolt out of here." Maxi turned towards Ric. "Start speaking French, very loud. Like we are arguing."

In perfect French, Ric recited, "No problem

there, mama." One of the soldiers walked over. "Are you American?" he asked.

"French American," Maxi answered in the best accent she could muster. Ric started speaking perfect French again. Maxi noticed her dad and Sam hanging back to watch the exchange. The soldier said something into a two-way radio.

"I am so sorry," he started to explain. "This boat is for Americans only. The French boat will be here later." He moved the group out of line. When Celia went to follow, he stops her.

"Sir, this is, er, my son's nanny," Maxi was quick to explain. "She must come to take care of the child." He gave Ev the staredown as she, in perfect Italian, told the soldier to screw off. Maxi's mouth opened and closed.

"Just go," said the soldier. The group moved out of view dodging in between anxious people. "That was close," Celia whispered. They walked to the backside of the casino. The car sat about ten blocks away, baking in the sunlight.

"Now, where are Sam and Rich?" Ev peered around the area.

"Right here," the sound of her husband's voice made everyone jump. "Did you receive a message from Zack?"

"Yes – what did Pete say?"

"Not to board the ship." Maxi nodded. "He said

we should head inland and try to find a place to stay for now. He didn't give details, just to call him when we were safe." In the distance, a gunshot echoed through the buildings, followed by shattered windows. Pressed up against the wall, Rich peaked around the corner to see a pair of soldiers shooting up their rental car. "On to plan B," he pointed down an alleyway to move the group away from the noise. Maxi watched her father put his arm around her mother and brush his lips against hers. "Did I really hear you tell the guy to screw off?" He laughed as her mother nodded.

"They are ruining our vacation," she said with a smirk.

"Mom, are we going to be okay?" Ric whispered. His sweaty hand hadn't left some part of Maxi for the last hour.

"Yes," Maxi said, hiding her face from his. Her other hand held her phone. The last check, she had less than a fifty percent charge. She had tried Zack back once they cleared the city, yet all she received was a voicemail for her efforts. Temptation beckoned her to try again, yet a diminishing battery power advised against. Her father had tried Pete, only to click into voice mail too.

They walked through the tall grass single file, heading in the general direction of Ayo Rock. The view of it from the garden of Madame

Jeannette's made navigation from the rock to several areas easy. The top would also give the landscape of their surroundings. Maxi hoped this would present options. The climb won't be easy. Maxi knew her mother hiked weekly back home, and she expected at least the two of them could walk to the top to describe the scene to the rest.

"We should bring water," Ric said to no one. "I'm thirsty."

"Me too, kid," her father responded. "Let's think about something else." Off in the distance stood La Cabana and The Marquis. Their path took the group in the opposite direction, heading more into the island's arid interior. When a deserted dirt road cut through the tall grass, Sam thought it might be a short cut to the restaurant.

"Head this way," he pointed to the clear path. With a shrug, all followed. Maxi's phone buzzed.

"Hello."

"Maxi...Maxi, is that you?"

"Zack?"

"Max, I can hardly hear you. Please listen. Do not board the boat for any reason. Head as far inland as possible. There are..."

"Zack?" Maxi repeated.

"What's going on?" her father and Sam asked at the same time.

"That was Zack," Maxi breath came in spirts, "He said to head inland, yet I couldn't catch the rest."
"Why inland?" Ev repeated. Maxi shrugged.
"I couldn't hear him," she said a bit too forcefully. The heat of the day had begun to wear.
"Let's move," Rich started to walk further into the tall grasses. Maxi caught the reflection of the blazing sun. Just yesterday, she appreciated its golden rays. At the same time, she lay on the beach, now as she clung to her son's hand while whispering prayers for safety, she resented its shine.
"I think we are close to the restaurant," Sam pointed towards a red, gold, and green flag hanging in the distance.

"So here is our current situation," Pete began. Zack recognized a few faces in the crowd, yet most of the dozen or so men present were a mystery to him. "The Navy captured two boats in our waters off Washington State. They drifted over while in the strait. A third vessel, who would not follow orders, has been destroyed." There was a hush throughout the room. "If we think our country as a giant square, three out of our four of our mainland borders are safe. There is no activity near Alaska, Hawaii, Guam, or others in outlying areas. The current concentration of activity is in the Southeast United States, yet most are in the Caribbean." A map went up behind him as Pete pointed to areas still of concern. "I should state upfront. This is also personal," he stared down each around the table. "My parents, sister, and nephew are presently on the island of Aruba." He waited for a beat before adding, "They were not passengers on the cruise ship that sank in international waters between Aruba and Curacao. As far as I know, they are somewhere in the middle of the island."

"I want to emphasize as always, my first priority is the security of our country. I brought in Agent Brady to assist on both issues. He has been in the family position before and brings extensive undercover experience. With any luck, in the future, he will be a permanent part of our team." Heads turn to nod in Zack's direction. Pete continued explaining the first phase of the plan. "Questions?"

"Is there a reason yet?"

"That is the question. We are hoping the west coast arrests will assist with getting to the objective. Next?"

"Did anyone contact Chavez?"

"Another good question. I believe the Secretary of State is involved, and we should hear his response as soon as there is information. Off the record, I don't think Chavez is involved."

"Why is that, boss?"

"If I say gut, you will all roll your eyes, so I will put it to you this way. Where is the gain, and how much would he be willing to give up to obtain it?" Heads began to nod. "Within Venezuela is some of the most beautiful beaches in the world. As far as I can figure, the islands do not have much else to offer.

Venezuela is oil and resource-rich on its own."
He waited for a beat before asking, "Other questions?"

"Could there be a Russia connection?"

Zack observed Pete glance over to the Admiral before responding, "No. Not at this time." The Admiral gave a slight nod in Pete's direction, rose, and left the room. Pete's eyes followed his moves before he continued with details of each person's goal and how it fit into accomplishing the overall plan.

Zack watched members nod. Some took notes old style, in little black memo books, while others typed into their government-issued cellphones. He noted he was the only one who appeared to practice active listening.

When finished, Pete scanned the room to eye each team member before dismissing the group. "You and your respective teams each have a job to execute. Remember to keep my office in the loop of any findings. We will be the central point for communications between all teams. Secure communications only moving forward, please." Zack sat and waited for the movement of chairs to cease. He observed men move towards the exit, making mental notes of who chatted with who, after along with which conversations started outside the room.

When the last person finished talking with

Pete, he stood to make his way towards his friend. A hand on the back of his shoulder stopped his forward movement.

"Zack Brady?" the stranger asked. Zack nodded. "I'm agent O'Malley." The hand was connected to a large man, who stood over six feet and, based on appearances, hit the gym. Zack glanced down at the I.D. that dangled near his heart: F.B.I. "I'm here—"

Zack held up both hands. He waited for the agent to nod before he reached into his bag, pulled out the laptop he used for work, and handed it over. "For this. I'll need a receipt." The other agent nodded and produced a typed document that listed only one item to be returned. Both he and Zack signed and dated the form, which was photographed with the agent's cellphone.

He extended his hand. "What are you going to do now?"

"Help my buddy out," Zack gave a head nod in Pete's direction, "and take a vacation I keep talking about."

"Best of luck to you," he took Zack's hand to shake as he pulled closer. "Spencer is pissed and on a tangent. I'd watch myself if I was you."

Zack nodded. "Thanks."

Pete watched the short interaction from a distance. He waited until the other agent, along with Zack's computer, left the room.

"Friend of yours?"
"Possibly. He just warned me to watch my back."
"Huh?"
"Nothing to worry about."
"What was so important on the laptop?"
"I'm not sure." Pete watched Zack. "I made copies of everything, and most of my work is in my safe or in a cloud so..." Zack looked over in time to catch Pete staring. "It's a habit I picked up from your sister. Saved both our asses too." He switched the focus back to their current task. "What's our plan?"
"I need to secure a group on the island. It isn't going to be easy since the only way we can see is coming in on the Venezuela side. Seas are rough and the terrain unforgiving."
"Isn't that where the natural bridge clasped a few years back?"
"Are you familiar with the area?"
"Not really. I thought it was interesting to promote a giant hole in a rock be such a draw for tourists." Pete laughed. "Who else is on the team? Since the Admiral was here, I assumed..." Zack watched Pete put the last paper in his briefcase and moved towards the door.
"He is involved on my end. Otherwise, it is a couple diver and you." Pete turned towards Zack and, in a hushed voice, "These bastards

blew up a cruise ship filled with innocent people. Your job is to move my family, and any other Americans left on the island to safety. We are in negotiation with a group that occupies the area near where you are landing. The current plan is to advance folks to the rendezvous point, and we will somehow airlift to a carrier floating in between Aruba and Venezuela."

"Got it." Zack hiked the strap of his bag to his shoulder. "I got through to Maxi yet could hardly hear her. I think your dad is in charge."

"What else is new?"

"And I think they are searching for friends on the island."

"My parents have been going long enough. They should be friendly with at least a few natives."

"I hope whoever they find, they are truly friends." Pete nodded in return.

"Zack, this isn't going to be easy. Chavez is quiet, and no one came forward to claim responsibility yet."

"I understand." Crowds parted as they made their way through the airport. Military police visible around each corner. Tired executives, harried travelers, and screaming children flash by as the exit draws closer. Pete slipped his badge into a reader as an unassuming door slid open. They walked into a gray, silent

hallway.
"We'll take a short cut over to our hanger."
They descended a flight of stairs. Pete lead through the silent maze. A few uniformed soldiers passed. As they did, they saluted both Pete and Zack.
"I keep thinking about Spencer. He wanted to know why I was accessing a Pentagon secured area. He told me to focus on my business. Why would he care?" Pete didn't say anything. "I wonder if any of this is connected."
"I don't know what to think at this point." He laughed. "I do know my mother is probably blaming Maxi for all this because she didn't take you along."
Zack cringed. "How is this her fault?"
"Well, you've met my mother." Zack nodded. "Actually, you've met my whole family."
"So that explains it?"
"Yeah – in Maxi's case, poor judgment. Bad choices. I could go on." Zack starts laughing. "You should have gone to Aruba, too, buddy." Pete slapped Zack's shoulder.
"It wasn't my choice. Besides your sister is—"
"Weird? Wacked? Pain in the ass? What?"
"Perplexing? Yes, that is the right word, perplexing."
"Perplexing, huh? I like pain in the ass better." Zack smiled. Pete hit a handle. As the door opened, the bright sunlight temporarily

blinded their way. Two figures approached, creating shadows, and reestablishing their vision. "Oh crap," Pete stated. "They probably won't accept your new I.D." Pete held up his hands.

Pete held his I.D. in front and waited. Zack did the same. Two men in camouflage carrying assault rifles blocked their path. Once Pete's badge is recognized, the two fell back into a salute. Pete salutes back.

"Sir, this is a restricted badge."

"He is with me," Pete explains.

"I understand, sir, yet this area is highly restricted. We can't—"

"I understand corporal, and we are on our way to obtain Agent Brady his correct credentials."

"Would you mind if we escorted you there?" This was not a question.

"I would appreciate it," Pete said. "Could you take us directly to Colonel Cogent's office? Agent Brady will be processed there." The M.P. nodded and led the group across the tarmac, past one fighter jet, a couple drones, through a makeshift pavilion lined with soldiers resting on their duffle bags, into a permanent warehouse quickly changed into formal offices. Zack noted the quick pace of the M.P. had the pair sitting in a reception area in under five minutes. Along the way, Pete continued to be saluted. Inside the pavilion, those who noticed the group stood at attention as he passed.

Zack also observed Pete showed little interest in the process as he quickly saluted to dismiss each as fast as he could. Zack considered busting his friend's ass yet thought better of it. There will be plenty of time later when they retold the story for the rest of their circle. Colonel Cogent's assistant moved the men from the waiting room to a small office with a big desk, and a larger man squeezed in behind it. He held a landline to his ear and one pudgy finger in the air as the two entered.

"Could you hold a moment, please," he cupped the phone and instructed his assistant,

"Louise, please take Mr. Brady to process for a new I.D."

"What division, sir?"

"Ours, of course." He said, "Ah, huh," into the receiver. He reverted his attention to adding, "Welcome aboard Brady. You are now part of the National Security team."

"Thank you, sir," Zack responded as he stood. Pete gave a head nod as Zack followed the uniformed female through a side door and down a bland hall. Zack was lead through a process consisting of electronic fingerprints, photo I.D. picture, and a retinal scan. As he entered the office, Colonel Cogent stood and offered his hand. Zack hung back to salute, and the Colonel waved him off.

Maximum Trouble

"Mr. Brady, welcome to the team," he bellowed as he again extended his hand. "Pete has been telling me about your attributes for years."

"Thank you, sir," Zack replied as he reached out to his new boss. He noted the Colonel's grip was firm yet not overpowering. A sign of a true leader, someone who is aware of his power, Zack quickly assessed. He sat down next to Pete as the two continued their conversation.

"According to passport scans and the size of the cruise ship that sank, we estimate there are at least five thousand Americans still on the island. Some are being held at hotels on hotel row on the north side and others, like your family, we are having trouble locating." Pete nodded. His face was unreadable.

"Do we have a reason yet?" he asked.

"No, but there is a theory. Intelligence indicates last month's drug bombing in the Congo killed the head of one of the largest cartels in the world. We think this is his survivor's version of revenge."

"Do you think a drug lord would have access to this much military surplus? We destroyed a U-boat and captured two others on the West coast plus the ships I observed in international waters—"

The colonel raised his chubby hand. "I see where you are going with this." He looked around his office and took a quick glance out the door. All three men leaned forward across his desk. "It is a theory. I'm not too keen on it, yet this is what Central Intelligence is saying." He leaned back and indicated the others to do the same.

"I sent my men out with orders. I got one team handling direct threats and going after the ships now off the Carolinas. The intel from the drones shows skeleton crews. My other team is heading to Florida to handle the situation going on in the waters between us and Cuba. My last team— "

"You and Mr. Brady here?"

"Actually, there are four more members. Will be dropped on the south side of the island. Our plan is to keep an aircraft carrier within a safe distance and helicopter rescue off the island. We can start on hotel row if you'd like."

"I'm not sure it will be that easy. Whoever this is, is in control of the island. As far as we can tell, their headquarters are in one of the central hotels. Also, there is a presence in both major cities. It looks like they are looking for someone or something, yet I can't figure out what."

"So, Chávez is out as a suspect?" Zack inquired.

"Yes, we actually spoke to his people, and they offered any support we needed. The Dutch government is in contact also. Both strongly suggested this is an American issue, and the United States needs to fix their mess and bring tranquility back to their island."

"Do we have any idea of why Aruba and not any of the other islands?"

"He's a thinker," the Colonel commented to Pete. "We now know there was some activity on Curacao last month. Their police dealt with it efficiently and did not let the situation leak to the press. These islands depend so much on tourism for their economy. Any safety issues could crush a season. Other than that, all other Caribbean islands are indicating no difficulties. Cruise ships diverted from the area, and the rebel group essentially shut down the airport."

"Sir, I understand rescuing our citizens is a top priority, yet I can't help to think about why? And the who? There needs to be more of a reason for all this then retaliation for a drug bust. Who on the island could either possess a threat or is an asset to the militants?"

"I am hoping you can discover that Mr. Brady. There is more to your team's mission than getting Americans, and all people, to safety. We need to figure out why this happened to make certain it doesn't happen again. Comprehend?" Zack and Pete shook their heads in agreement. "Your ride is ready when you are."

The two stood and exited the office. Neither

spoke as they walked towards one of the hangers. Both lost in their own thoughts.

Maximum Trouble

"Thank heavens, you are safe," the same host as the night before ran up to greet their small party, his smile replaced with worry lines. A clap of his hands brought pitchers of water and glasses. In between swallows, echoes of "Thank you" reverberated.

"I heard about the boat…"

"What about the boat?" Sam and Rich exchanged glances.

"Oh, you did not hear the boom?" Maxi thought back to when they were walking through the grass. What sounded like an explosion had vibrated in the distance. "The cruise ship…"

No one spoke for a moment. Ric disengaged his hand and started to move towards the restaurant's interior. "Ric?" Maxi called.

"I got to" he jerked his head in the direction of the men's room.

"Oh," Maxi hesitated. "Me too," she started to follow.

"Mom you know I am old enough—"

"I know. I forgot I had to," she pushed on the door with a woman's silhouette painted in the middle. As Maxi sat, she could hear a flushing noise from the men's room and the door open then close. A moment later, she heard a voice coming through the wall.
"We must help them," a man's voice stated. "They have been friends for years."
"Not friends, customers," a female voice corrected.
"Okay, customers. But still, we should help."
"We can't. They said—"
"The hell with them. These are people in trouble." Maxi waited as the silence grew.
"Okay. We get them to the house, and then they are on their own," the female instructed. "And you must not tell them anything," she cautioned.
Maxi waited a few minutes before flushing the toilet. She walked back to see her group seated in the garden. The host in the middle of an explanation. She quietly joined in the back, yet when she and the host made eye contact, he shot daggers back, for a second. One of Maxi's hands instinctively reached for Ric. The other stroked the back of her neck.
I hope he really is a friend.

"Oh, crap!"
"Maxi, what's wrong?" Like a magnet to steel,

her mother came to her side. Maxi stood, staring at her phone.

"Crap, Crap, Crap," she muttered.

"Mom, are you alright?" Ric's furred brow appeared in her vision.

"Yeah, honey," Maxi replied as she rubbed his shoulder. "My freakin' phone—"

"Mary Alexis!"

"Just freakin' died!" Ric shook his head.

"Don't you own a charger?" Her mother said, adding, "Really, Maxi, you should always bring a charger."

"I do own a freakin' charger," Maxi snapped back.

"Well, good – then everything is fine." Her mother threw her arms up in the air while she stomped in the direction of her husband.

Under her breath, Maxi muttered, "Of course I own a freakin' charger in my freakin' suitcase in the freakin' car freakin downtown with the freakin' hoodlums." Maxi sucked in a deep breath and caught a snicker escape from Ric's direction. She focused her eyes on her son, who returned her glare with an exaggerated eye roll.

"Really, mom," he voiced his disbelief.

"Maxi, your mother said your phone is out of juice?" Maxi nodded back at her dad. "Okay, then. I'll turn mine off for now. We'll figure out how to charge up later."

Maxi shared a slight smile in her dad's

direction. The late-day sun left burn marks across any exposed skin. Ric's bright red neck had Maxi make a mental note to find some aloe for him as they walked.

"Simon said to head in this direction, and he would send someone to pick us up and give a place to stay." Maxi nodded as she heard a loud huff expel from her mother's mouth.

"Look hon, this is the best we got," her dad started to explain before throwing his hands up in the air.

"Are we going to be okay, mom?" Ric whispered. Maxi put her arm around her son and gave him a hug.

"We are going to be fine, although we may be extending our vacation a bit." Ric squeezed Maxi's hand. She turned in the other direction to avoid him seeing the water in her eyes.

Maxi and Ric lagged behind the group. Her dad and Sam had taken the lead while she could hear her mom and Celia talking about nothing. The flowers on the trail are beautiful. I wonder what they are. Oh look, there's a rabbit.

If the situation was different, this could be a family hike, except her father didn't hike, and judging what she knew about Sam, he was a stranger to mother nature too.

Her mom walked every day, and she knew her dad went to the gym at least three times a week. Despite their decent shape, both were in their early 70's. Not a great combination for walking in the heat. Ric at least played outside and loved to run. While her mind wandered, she decided the cramp in her thigh, made her, the youngest adult, the one in the worst shape.

Now that was funny. So funny to Maxi, she started laughing. Laughing so forceful, Rich and Sam stopped in their tracks. While the others turned to see what the joke is, Ric watched his mother. His hand stayed connected to hers, yet his eyes reached out to his grandparents to do something.

"Maxi," she heard her mother's voice. "Maxi are you—"

"I'm fine, mom," she said between giggles. "I just can't stop."

The loud growl of the engine gave Zack moments to think. Crammed inside the cavern of the airplane, he sat surrounded by ten strangers, each having their own stake in what happens next. The plan sounded simple enough...drop into the waters on the south side of the island. Swim to shore. Set up a small, indiscreet base and round up people to transfer back via helicopter or offshore boat. That is his objective.

Four others are part of the extraction team. The rest are on a different mission. Pete didn't say what the purpose is, yet Zack had been a part of enough teams to understand they are going after the cause. He didn't have the details, he prayed the two plans to fail to intersect.

"Yo," dressed in camouflage, they all are supposed to appear alike, yet even in fatigues and face paint, Zack knew Rod's presence.

"Yo, yourself," he responded.

Maximum Trouble

Rod's shrill could be heard over the rumble, yet quiet enough for the rest not to hear. "I have an idea for finding Maxi and company," he stated, "Based on what Pete had shared in the briefing, we can assume they are not holed up on hotel row." Zack nodded in agreement, "So I'm thinking we should steal, er, borrow a vehicle and head into the brush. We can worry about the others after—"

Zack held his hand up. "I appreciate you wanting to go for Pete's—"

"And yours—"

"Family first yet since there isn't a clear picture of the situation as yet. At this point, I think we should stick to the plan."

"But we may not—"

"We should stick to the plan," Zack's voice did not waver. Rod focused on him for a beat before giving a single nod. "We good?"

"Yes." Zack cringed as Rod's hand flew into a salute. He regretted he had somehow been recommissioned at his old rank. The other guys think he is in charge when that couldn't be further from the truth. Yes – there is a side effort …

Zack let out an audible sigh. He needed to focus. His eyes closed to visualize the jump. He saw himself swimming to shore. Based on satellite photos they had, the best location for a camp appeared over the hill by the old natural bridge. The other team would set up nearby in the same area. Several concerns floated by, yet Zack attempted to squelch each with simple logic. *The people of Aruba want peace. They will be helpful. They are landing on the opposite side of the island. Guards, if any, will be few. Sharks!* Zack laughed. There is no answer to that one.

He visualized the other team providing some sort of barrier around their base camp, so they could leave people there in between runs. Maybe instead of a helicopter, one of the speed boats from the carrier could be used to move people. He could see a lot of civilians milling around the carrier.

An ear-splitting bell jilted Zack awake. He stretched forward to position his gear to not fly out of reach. As big as an aircraft carrier appears, there is only a certain amount of runway. The jerk of the plane at the end is one of the few movements that raise his awareness. As a seaman, he watched an inexperienced pilot put an F-16 fighter jet into the Gulf of Mexico. All had survived, yet not without many future nightmares. He gripped his backpack to wait for the pull.

The landing was the worst, yet the alternative didn't work much for him either.

Maximum Trouble

The regular *Seafood Grill's* lunch crowd dwindled down to two men, one dreadlocked, dressed in a Hawaiian shirt and red Bermuda shorts and the other in a full formal tuxedo. Men in black carrying AK-47's stood in each corner.

The few staff who remained attended to both the men at the table, along with their guards on the outskirts. They continuously filled water glasses, plates of fresh fruits and vegetables, and portions of grilled fish, caught that morning.

Once the glasses filled and plates overflowing, most of the staff are ushered off of the deck. The beautiful sea view is dampened only by the ominous gray vessel in the center. The men mirror each other in taking a few bites of the fish. Both sit back in the chairs. The sun blazes down.

"You have done an excellent job preparing the island," the man in the tuxedo began. "Yet, you failed to find our targets."

"Thank you for your compliment, sir. We have—" The tuxedo man's hand raises.

"I do not need excuses. My people need results. My contact in the U.S. insists the codes are on this island. I was told, for some reason, it is felt safer for three to four people to have access to the sequence. I don't understand," he threw his hands in the air.

"Do we have a name yet? It would make the process easier."

"If I had a name, would I need you?" Tuxedo man gazed around his companion at one of the guards who returned a smile. "Ah, one word. A gesture even."

"Excuse me?"

Tuxedo man brought his attention back. "Nothing," he swatted the air. "Nothing to worry." His smile didn't reach his eyes. "We got rid of most of the tourists. The rest are either in this tower or hiding. It is the ones who hide I worry about." The other man nodded.

"I brought you more today."

"Yes. Yes, you did. I give trustworthy information. There are more. Perhaps a family, multigenerational, traveling together? One carries the codes."

"Boss, if you don't mind me asking, what are these codes?"

Maximum Trouble

"I do mind, but I will tell you anyway. My people acquired two of the codes to launch explosives from the United States. With the third component, we can start a world war. But here's the best part," laughter echoes above the calypso beat, "the United States takes the blame. They will be attacked. They lose!"

"Huh." Not for the first time, Talin wondered if his partner oversimplified or was downright crazy.

"And you, my friend," now more boisterous, "go after what should be yours." He swept his hands around the room as if the cloudless sky, blue ocean, and island paradise are his to give. Tuxedo man laughed. "As soon as I receive what will be mine."

He leaned forward across the table, dropped his voice to above a whisper, "Go find what is mine." Talin nodded as he rose to leave. He watched the guards move their rifles from resting to point at him as he moved to the exit. His prize will be mighty if he could complete this task.

Tuxedo man waited for the exit before he gave the host a quick nod. The guard closest handed over a cellphone as the others moved out of view. He waited until the room emptied before pushing the buttons.

Skipping pleasantries', he asked, "Do you have a name?" and waited.

A woman's voice responded, "Only the ones I already gave you."

"Malone and Jacobs do not have the codes, correct?"

"No, but they are related to someone who can secure them." She waited for a beat before adding, "There may be a problem."

"I don't like problems." Her arms got bumpy in the silence.

"My contact left the office. I lost my security access."

"So, you are useless?" The response slapped her in the face.

"I am never useless." She waited for a reply, adding, "I will figure it out. Same deal?"

"Yes, of course." He started to hang up before asking, "Who was your in-office contact to the system?"

"Zack Brady."

"And where is this Zack Brady's whereabouts?"

"My guess would be D.C."

"Perfect." He thanked her, assuring they would be in touch soon, before disconnecting. He punched in another number. "See what you could find about Zack Brady and if you can discover where he is, even better."

Upon entering the third number, "I got

another name, Zack Brady. If he is on the island, kill him."

Maxi followed her mother into the small van. The sign on the side read Paradise Motel and Spa. Ric climbed upon his mother's lap inside the area designated for luggage. "All set?" she heard her father ask. A ripple of "Yes" followed.

The van started with a jerk. The driver smiled and nodded towards Simon. He waved out the window while maneuvering down the dirt driveway.

"Ow!" Ric exclaimed. The sound of his head hitting the roof echoed. Maxi tried to squish her body down to give him more headroom. The van swirled through a cornfield, up into a desert area.

"I avoid roads," the driver explained.

"Good idea," Rich said.

"What part of the island are we going to?" Sam asked. He had been unusually quiet during their visit to the restaurant. His wife was equally silent.

Maximum Trouble

"Opposite the hotel row. I am taking you to my cousin's place." Rich learned long ago cousin was a broad term used for those close. Sometimes they were related yet most of the time not. He relaxed a little in his seat and let out a slow breath. The day had been hectic. Rich turned on his phone to see one text message. It read, "hold tight, dad. We are coming to find you."

He turned his phone off and placed it back in his shirt pocket. Glancing at the driver, Rich decided to wait with the news. Pete would be here soon. In his mind, they were safe.

The strip motel rested in the middle of an overgrown garden. The place had seen better days. The paint on the cement cracked. Vegetation grew up on the sides of the building. The van stopped inside the gate. The driver hopped out and spoke to someone in a rapid combination of island creole and Spanish.

"More Americans? Where am I to put these?"

"He wants to know what he's supposed to do?" Ric interpreted. "He's not angry, at least he doesn't act it," he added. Maxi rubbed her son's back and tried to move her legs. They had cramped up at the first hard left. They watched the driver walk back.

"Ok, you can go," he instructed with a smile.

"Go where?" Sam asked.

"Here is your new place now. My cousin,

Phillipe, and his family run it, and he will take care of you. For now."

The group moved out of the van at a cautious pace. Phillipe lead through a large arch. Maxi swatted spiders, both real and imaginary, as she followed. Inside, the courtyard sparkled. Reflections of the sun bounced off the in-ground pool area, catching several people positioned on plastic lounge chairs. The stillness interrupted only by the occasional splash. No screams of joy or laughter of jokes. People greeted their group with slow smiles and nods.

They followed Phillipe down a path to a lone bungalow. Inside an older woman sat peeling plantains. He said something in Spanish, and she nodded in return. Maxi noted whatever would happen, it happened by agreement of all. A small man, perhaps an older version of Phillipe, appeared from another room.

"Greetings," he said. His voice low. "welcome to The Paradise. You are friends of Simon, no?"

"Yes – we are friends of Simon," Rich repeated.

"I can only give you one room. That is all it is left. There are rules here," he waited for the group to gather closer. "We do not draw attention to the property. There is no yelling or loud noises. Men are required to participate in the nightly watch. This means walking around the parameter for a couple hours each night. My son Phillipe and I do the midnight to four shift because this is when the night animals come out. We are used to them," he shrugs.

"Women can help my wife cook, if you choose, or clean up. You are responsible for your own room. There is no maid service. Washers are provided. Sun is our dryer. All clothes, sheets, and such, must be out of view by days end." He watched each facial expression. "For now, you will be safe here. We will keep you posted on island conditions. As far as we are aware, all activity is still centered around hotel row and our capital. There is no response from your government."

No one said a word. Each looked to the other for next moves. "Rich, can I see you outside for a minute?" Sam moved towards the door. "Just a minute," he added. Once out of earshot, "Did you notice around the pool?" Rich nodded. "I only saw two men, yet they both sported marine tattoos."

"Marine tattoos?"

"Yeah, the Semper fi thing with the eagle."

"Huh."

"For now, I think we are okay here, yet we need to figure out how to get off this island."

"I agree. My son sent a text he is coming for us. We need to lay low until he gets here." They walked back into the office. "We'll take the room and sleep in shifts. There are six of us."

"Phillipe will assist with your luggage—"

"Our luggage is in our rental cars downtown. By now, it's probably been stolen."

"I will find you clothes at the church. They won't be new or designer, but they will cover your behinds," he said.

"What does the room cost?" Ev said. When she got an eye roll from her husband, she added, "Someone needed to ask."

"As long as you help out with the chores, the room is free or by donation once you are safely home. Until then, please accept our hospitality during these strange times."

Echoes of thank you filled the room, followed by a shush. Moving as one, they followed Phillipe back down the path. He walked to the place on the left end and opened the door. Maxi noted no key used. The musty smell floated out. Phillipe moved across the area to open shades. A large floor to ceiling window gave a view out to the pool area. The room appeared decent size with two large beds, a dresser, a television with an antenna out the back, and on the opposite wall, another smaller window, frosted over. The bathroom had the standard toilet, sink, and shower.

"This is lovely," Celia exclaimed. The rest of the group agreed.

"Get settled and find me when you want to go

to the church. It isn't far," Phillipe left to a chorus of thank you.

They waited until the Phillipe moved past the front window. Ric stared out at the pool and back at his mother, who sat on the edge of the far bed. "Take a quick shower, and you can go in your shorts for now," Maxi answered his unasked question.

As Ric moved towards the bathroom, he stopped in front of his grandma, "See why she scares me at times," his voice soft enough for all to hear. The bathroom door closed, and the shower could be heard.

The adults gathered in a circle. "We need to find other clothes," Ev pointed out.

"Always the shopper," Rich joked.

"I just—" Her husband embraced her.

"It's okay," Sam jumped in. "We should get at least a change of clothes. I think we need to find out more about this place, too."

Maxi sat back on the bed and watched the exchange. Although the conversation is hushed, each, who spoke, glanced back between the window and the group. Ric exited the shower to lay down on the bed in between. Yesterday the family enjoyed a tropical vacation; today, an oppressive nightmare. She listened to her father and Sam go back and forth, as they debated the best approach.

"My son texted to sit tight. Hopefully, they are on their way. If we are safe here—" The knock on the door had all jump. Phillipe smiled and waved from the window.

"Are you ready?" We want to go before nightfall." He held up the van keys in his hand.

"Yes, Phillipe. Please give us a minute." Phillipe vanished down the path.

"Ric is tired," Maxi said. All turned in her direction, wide-eyed. "We'll stay here, take a nap..."

"Or swim," Ric whispered.

"Or swim," she clarified. Ric stammered back towards the bathroom. "We can stay here. I think we'll be all right. See if anyone here owns a phone charger?"

"Useful idea, Max," her father agreed. "I would prefer to leave someone else here with you."

"I'll stay," Sam volunteered. Celia jumped. "Don't worry, honey. Besides, you buy all my clothes anyway."

"Okay, now it is settled." Ev followed her husband out the door with Celia close behind. The distant splash of water providing the only sound.

"Don't mind me," Sam started to explain.

"No worries. Ric and I are going to hang by the pool." She watches her parents disappear around the corner. "The kid needs a break." Sam nodded. He stayed behind as Maxi and Ric walked across the courtyard towards an empty lounge chair. She spread her towel over the top of what appeared to be a green mold and let her body sink down.

Ric walked over to the edge of the pool and put his toe in. Maxi watched her son debate between going all-in or morphing slow. With a splash, a shower of water descends on her legs. A few minutes later, Maxi heard the familiar sound of laughter coming from her son as another child invited him to play Marco Polo. Her hand wiped the mystery tear, moving down her cheek. *This had to be okay,* she told herself. Zack's face flashed for a moment, and Maxi promptly shook him off. *He can't save me twice.*

The van swiveled down a dirt road, bumping over roots and holes, to send the occupants flying in their seats. A collective gasp released as Phillipe barreled through seagrass to bring the vehicle to a quick stop against a white building.

"Come, come," he directed the group around the side to a discreet entrance. The small church appeared simple. A dozen or so benches faced a small raised area. Standard large wood carved cross on the back wall. The cross decorated with vines of flowers. Phillippe moved to the opposite side and led the group through an archway. In the vestibule, several boxes sat overflowing with clothes.

"Please," Phillipe indicated. Ev walked over to

the first box and started to sort through the contents, which consisted of mostly outdated resort wear. As she began to piling its contents according to size, Celia followed suit. Rich stood and watched.

"You could help," She pointed to a third box in the corner. Rich started to pick through its contents when he pulled out a familiar shirt. "Hey," he exclaimed, getting the attention of all. He held a shirt that read *I'm Retired – Go Around.* "It's my size too." Phillippe clapped. "Good fortune, no?"

"No. This is some of our luggage." Phillippe frowned.

"Mr. Rich," he started to speak. "We did not..." he sputtered. "I mean, we need to help..." Phillippe threw his hands up and started talking a combination of island creole and rapid Spanish. While he paced, Rich pulled out a few more shirts and shorts. "We..."

"Phillippe," Ev went to his side. "We do not think you stole our things. Finding it all is our good luck," she said.

Phillippe stopped pacing. "Yes – good luck. But we need to help many," He gestured towards the boxes.

"We will only take what's necessary," Celia injected. Ev nodded in agreement while Rich shook his head.

"But," he pointed to the contents of their

luggage.

"Only what is necessary," Ev repeated. She watched her husband dig deep within the box, soon discovering its only contents to be clothing.

"Damn,' he said to no one. "No charger." Ev and Celia collected two sets of clothes per person in the party, including an actual bathing suit for Ric. They packed everything into a paper bag, provided by Phillippe.

"Thank you for leaving a donation," he gushed. "Mr. Rich, are you mad?"

"Oh no, Phillippe. I didn't find something. I thought we'd be lucky."

"You already got lucky, no?" Rich held up his phone and pointed to where the charger would fit.

"I need a charger."

"I find you one. I promise."

"Thank you, Phillippe."

"We need to move." The group went back to the van, which Phillippe backed into the seagrass and towards the hotel.

Maxi closed her eyes for a minute, and a shadow fell to block the late day heat remaining in the sun. "What Ric?" she replied with a sigh.

"Oh – sorry," and unfamiliar voice answered. Maxi opened one eye to catch a shadow sporting a bikini and a huge pale blue sun hat.

"Sorry," she sat up too quickly. Black dots formed and faded. "Thought you were my son."
"He's playing with mine in the pool. I'm Gigi." Maxi watched as the woman glanced back over her shoulder before she squatted next to her chair. "I'm American too," she whispered. Maxi nodded and waited. "We were on vacation, my husband, kid, and I when a friend of his called and warned us to leave the island. We moved back here yesterday, but my husband went back to our villa for his computer..."
"Where is your husband now?"
Gigi choked. In a low voice, she said, "I don't know." Maxi watched her wipe her eyes with her hand. "He left last night because we were told it would be safer for him. I don't know why he needed his computer so bad or why he didn't bring it in the first place. He had locked it in the safe so no one else could retrieve it. This is so frustrating!"
Maxi gave the woman a quick hug and added, "I'm sorry. We were vacationing too. A friend of my dad's brought us here." She stopped to glance at the two kids playing in the pool. Gigi's splashed in circles while Ric sported a furrowed brow. Maxi gave a quick smile in his direction, relieved when his shoulders released. "My mom and dad and their friend

went to find clothes at the church. We only have what we are wearing..."

Gigi composed herself and sat down. "There is another family here too. Not sure if they are Americans. I saw them go into one of the villas in the back. The guys were out here earlier but left while you all were inside. Otherwise, it's us. God, I wish Walter would come back!"

Maxi kept watch passed Gigi to the entrance and silently wished for her parents to come back too.

Pete watched the four computer screens in front of him. He put the volume up on the one directly in front of him. Two men sit at a rectangular table in metal folding chairs. The room appeared a faded green with no doors or windows visible, only the two-way mirror with shadows passing behind. Neither man moved or spoke.
On the screen, military police lead a group of men with their hands above their heads down a dock. Pete counted six prisoners. He noted the time and place scribed on the bottom. Pensacola Florida. The crew from the last boat in U.S. waters finally arrived at the base. This will bring beneficial news, he hoped.
Back to the first screen, still no movement.
"For crying out loud," he muttered.
"Still nothing," Commander Atwood's voice caught him off guard.
"They brought the crew in from the boat off Florida. This guy," he pointed to screen one, "is sitting there. They've been like this for the

past hour."

"What about North Carolina?"

Pete watched the third screen. "Nothing. Just a big blue ocean." The Colonel nodded. "The only other place I am tapped into is our ship between Venezuela and Aruba."

"Anything?"

"They are on board and ready to take the launch. So far, zero activity in the area, both in the ocean and on the side of the island, we'll be landing."

"Island intel is the same. Best we can figure, most Americans are in two of the high rises on hotel row; the Divi and the Sea View. Both properties are owned by locals. From what we can see, all American owned properties are shut down. The Marriott had two villas explode earlier. We do not believe anyone was hurt."

"Are the rebels still headquartered at the airport?"

"We believe so. Team two is instructed to head in that direction upon landing."

"I hate the wait."

"Me too."

"I should have gone."

"Pete, we can't have emotions in the way of duty. That is why we—"

"Brought Zack in. Although speaking of emotions…"

"Zack will get the job done. He understands

his role..."

Maximum Trouble

Zack brought his pack to his shoulder. He stood to exit. Black spots vaporized his vision. His body folded back into the seat. Landing sickness. He hadn't suffered from it in years. He took in a few deep breaths and waited. Nausea should pass soon. The thumps of heavy footsteps keep his mind in the present. He visualized each man lifting their pack and placing one strap across their shoulder. He pictured the slow-moving line towards the exit. The salt air was hitting their senses as they departed aboard the deck.

When the sounds faded, Zack lifted his body to a standing position, this time no spots. He slung his backpack over his shoulder to start to walk the length of the plane. His team waited on deck, ready for the next part of their journey.

"Change of plans, sir," Rod said.

"What kind of changes?"

"We are taking the amphibious vehicle to the shore. The Captain thinks we can move people

back more efficiently…"
"Anything else?"
"Not that I am aware of."
"Thanks for the update." Zack turned away from the group and took his satellite phone from the pack. Without salutation, he asked, "Change of plans?"
"News to me," Pete answered.
"Amphibious versus speed boat?"
"I'll check," Zack observed his team while he waited. Rod stood center holding court. The rest was laughing along to his punchlines. The captain disappeared yet, there appeared to be eyes on Zack from all angles. His fingers wrapped around the friendship bracelet in his pocket. Just purple and blue string tied together yet its touch brought back memories of a few weeks ago, the town fair with Maxi and Ric. Maxi insisted all three had matching bracelets and spent too much time making sure of it, in his and Ric's opinion.
At the time, Zack refused to wear it. Told her straight out, "this is way too hippy-dippy," yet now he keeps it tucked into his pants pocket.
"Yeah," he heard Pete's voice with static.
"Apparently, the speed boat is not working," Pete enunciated his words with clarity, "so the Captain came up with the alternative." Zack opened his mouth to respond as Pete continued in a dropped voice, "Zack, do what

you need to do. Once you land to break off from the team, take someone you trust with you if possible. We just got word, my parents, along with several others, are holed up in an old motel in the center of the island. The place is guarded, yet we don't think they are being held hostage at this point."

"How did you find them?"

"You are going to laugh – My dad's old cellphone has a tracker on it."

"You're kidding me."

"I wish I was. My dear sister probably turned hers off, yet my dad, who is tech-deficient, never bothered to set his security levels. Zack, there is one thing—"

"If we can find him, others can too?"

"Exactly."

"I'll pull Rod aside. Strange, he actually pitched breaking off to find the family on the way over. I'll see what his plan is. I will also make certain the rest of the team heads to the other side to start evacuating people. We can move a whole lot more through on the amphibian."

"I was thinking about this. Keep your tracker on so we can note your progress. Channel C-5."

"Got it – out." Zack walked back towards the group, who stopped laughing with his approach. "Am I the butt of this joke?" he casually inquired. He waited for someone to

respond, and when no one did, he continued, "The boat is broken, so plans needed to be changed. Do what you need to do – we leave in two hours. Any questions?"
"Same plan," Rod asked.
"Same plan," Zack answered.

Maxi wandered back to the room. She found Sam sitting on the bed with pieces of paper scattered around him. He stared down at the pile.

"Waiting for a miracle," Maxi asked. She positioned herself, so she could watch Ric, who tossed a Frisbee with Gigi's son outside their room and to observe what Sam was doing.

"Nope," he answered without taking his eyes off the arrangement. "I am looking for patterns.

"Patterns?"

"Yes – patterns and if the various situations intersect, all the better."

Maxi nodded. "I remember Zack talking about patterns." She started to read Sam's notes. "He explained every circumstance contains certain conditions surrounding it—"

"And those conditions dictate what will happen next or in this case, possibly what the overall goals of the culprit would be. If I can

figure that out—"
"Then we can find a way out."
"Yes!" Both Sam and Maxi stared at the pile. Maxi moved a few notes around only to shake her head and pushed the paper back to their original positions. The Frisbee bounced off the window. Both jumped.
"Just me," Ric said as he retrieved the disc and waved.

Phillippe turned the van towards the dirt road at the same time two men in camouflage emerged from the brush. "Hold your tongues," Phillippe muttered as the men approached the van. Rich noted both carried military-grade semi-automatic rifles along with a sidearm and knife. Both sported green and black paint across their faces. "Buenos Dias," Phillippe said in perfect Spanish.
"Good morning," the soldier responded in broken English. "What's going on here?"
"Just taking a few folks to church," Rich watched Phillippe cross his fingers under the steering wheel.
"Church, huh?"
"Yes – there is a Christin church and cemetery passed the grass."
"And this is the road to the church?" Rich observed the other man as he walked around the van. He soon appeared at his passenger

side window. Neither spoke.

"This is a short cut. My village is over the bend that way," Phillippe pointed in the opposite direction of the hotel. "We were heading back after praying for peace this morning."

The soldier smiled. "Well, I guess today is your lucky day," he said.

"Why is that?" Phillippe asked.

"Because you are going to drive us to our church where you all can pray with the rest of your kind."

The soldier indicated for Phillippe to step out of the van, which he complied with. The soldier followed him around the back. The gunshot came quick.

Rich watched the second soldier. His facial expression stayed neutral. "You drive," the soldier indicated for Rich to move over. He wedged his body into the driver's seat and caught Ev's eye in the rear-view mirror. Her face stayed stoic, yet the color of her pupils had turned to black. She sat still, hands folded on her lap. Celia mirrored her pose. The hatchback flung open, and the van creaked as the second soldier positioned his body in the back.

"Vamoose!" he instructed. Rich felt the barrel of the gun in his side. He brought the van into gear and turned the wheels to follow where his passenger pointed. *Dear father, please welcome Phillippe into your kingdom. He died in service to others...*

Maximum Trouble

Zack wandered down to the commissary and grabbed a turkey sandwich off the shelf. He found an empty table off to the side, away from the rest of the crew. His next steps would be crucial. He needed someone to assist, yet the recoiling in his gut told him to avoid Rod.

The rest of the crew were new entities. He wasn't familiar with skill levels or areas of expertise. He did recognize both Pete and Commander Atwood had qualified each member for the team function at maximum capacity. This became his challenge. Who could he collaborate with that wouldn't affect the overall mission in a negative capacity by interrupting their part in the plan?

Deep in thought, he took large bites of his sandwich, swallowing each without chewing. Pete's latest communication bothered him. Rich's cellphone, along with Rich they presume, is now moving cross-island towards hotel row. That could only mean they were captured and are being transferred.

Zack did not like the alternative scene that came up in his imagination. If Pete's family is being relocated, the militants are still in the dark. If their identity is discovered, Zack shuttered. Emotional involvement on any mission could get one killed.

When his crew got up to leave, the level of movement rocked him out of his contemplations. He went too, bringing the second half of his sandwich along with him.

"That meat will kill you," his movement interrupted by a giant. The man in front of him sported a Hawaiian shirt and Bermuda shorts. He stood at least six inches taller than Zack.

"What can you do?" Zack shrugged and went to walk around.

The man leaned in, "I can kill a man with my hands." Zack repositioned his gear to free up one arm. The man exploded in laughter. "My god, you should see your face. Ken Boci," he extended his hand to shake.

"Zack Brady," for a large guy, he possessed a gentle handshake. "And I'll take my chances with any ship food." This got another boisterous laugh in return. "New Navy uniform?"

"Naw – I want to fit in with the natives when we land."

"We?" Zack tilted his head to one side. The

gesture mimicked by the giant.

"The person in charge is always the last to find out," Ken laughed. In a much quiet voice, "Dude, I'm your wingman. Commander Atwood changed my duties to help you guys."

Zack hesitated, "Welcome aboard. What is your function?"

Ken's laughter echoed in the room. "Well, I already gave away my basic skill set." Zack waited without expression. "The reason I'm your wingman is that I am acquainted with the island. My family lived there for five years right before I graduated high school and joined the Navy. Also, unlike you, I have the security clearances to obtain help if we should need it. From what I have been briefed about your M.O., you will probably call Pete Malone or one of the others to dig up the goods on me, so you might as well go outside and take care of that." Ken waited, yet Zack did not move. "The sooner you do, and we both know you will, the sooner we can sketch out a plan to get your gal and her family to safety. Oh, and so you are aware, I am in the loop; when you call, ask about Pete's father and his whereabouts. We need to move."

Zack turned and walked out to the flight deck. He stood back to watch the crew loading up AV-1 (Amphibious Vehicle One) with supplies: food and ammunition, what else could they possibly need? He dialed into Pete and waited.

When the phone went to voicemail, he hung up and dialed again. On the third attempt, he answered.

"Patience is a virtue you obviously do not possess," Pete answered, out of breath.

"Something you forgot to tell me?" Zack tried to remain calm.

"Not my idea," Pete said.

"Look, you made it clear I am not in charge—"

"But, you're uncomfortable with this..."

"Exactly."

"Zack, my father's cellphone, has a tracker on it and about a half-hour or so ago his phone started to head towards hotel row. For the last five minutes, the beacon pulsed from one of the high rises. If my family is at a high rise—"

"We need to move fast."

"Agent Boci, he is Central Intelligence and at one time part of Naval Special Forces—"

"Seals?"

"No, different division yet close. Marine trained."

"Respect."

"No, shit. He's lived on the island. His current address is a few islands over. He is still very familiar with the area. Says he knows people throughout the Caribbean."

"Everyone needs friends."

"Yes. Yes, we do. I got you and Boci taking a more undercover approach here, less direct than the others. I'd like frequent reports. I think we have a connection, and it's not good." Zack didn't ask, so Pete continued. "Any questions?"

Zack responded, "No, sir." He gave Pete a fake salute.

"I'm sending you a map that shows where the high rise appears to be about where the signal started. Zack, do what you do."

Zack pressed the end and waited for the buzz sound to indicate he had the map. The signal started in an area not far from their predicted landing, close to the run-down motel where they were heading. The route the phone followed, appeared direct to the tourist side of the island. The signal moved fast. "In a vehicle," Zack muttered. He focused on the map, closed his eyes, and moved his head in a circle. Upon opening his eyes, again, he brought his attention back to the map. He moved his head in a circle in the opposite direction. He saw zero evidence Rich was actually with his phone.

Zack turned to face the opposite direction, flipped his phone to study the same map. After the second sequence, he deleted the map. He turned back towards AV-1 and promptly walked into Ken Boci. "Jesus," Zack muttered.

"Did you receive this?" Ken held up his phone, revealing the map Zack had memorized.

"No, let me see," Zack reached for Ken's phone. Ken knocked his hand away.
"Wait, let me..." Ken pressed a button on his phone and looked back at Zack. "You're just, what? Testing me?"
"Is that what this is?"
"You tell me," with his arms folded across his chest, Agent Boci's presence grew.
Zack brushed off the slight. "Do we have a plan?" he asked as he mimicked Agent Boci's pose.
"Get off the boat. Go to the high rise. Get Pete's family, along with Commander Atwood's," Ken stopped. "They didn't tell you?"
Zack shook his head. "Last report I saw, which came in about a half-hour before you landed," Zack blew out his breath. It appeared his lack of inclusion is based on timing and not rank, "it said they estimate there are five thousand tourists on the island with about a quarter being American."
"Are the others allowed to leave?"
"A grounded Air Canada jet left today for Toronto. The rebels guaranteed it safe passage as long as there are no U.S. landings. If the plane lands in the United States, the rebels said they will not be responsible for the outcome. Last I heard the plane crossed into Canadian airspace outside Niagara and should land soon."

"How many were on board?"

"It was a big plane; five hundred and thirty, I think. All had Canadian passports." Zack nodded. "As far as the Americans go, the bulk of them are at the Divi on hotel row. Rich's phone stopped at the Sea View next door. There are people there. We think this is a mix of rebels and others. I don't have confirmation Rich is actually there, and if he is, who he is with."

"What about the others?"

"The first party is going to head in the direction of the airport. We think this is their headquarters. Our counterparts will head to the high rise…"

"But you have a different idea," Ken nodded.

"Well…"

"I think we should go where the signal starts. According to the map, we'd need a vehicle to move across the island anyway. Maybe someone is hiding information."

"We start at the beginning," Zack agreed. He started to walk in the direction of AV-1.

"Yo – Zack," Zack turned, "Did you really not receive this map?"

Zack laughed, "Are you really Naval Special Forces?"

"Touché."

Ev and Celia bounced around as Rich attempted to drive the van through a dirt path. They moved in the opposite direction of the motel. The soldiers laughed harder with each bounce. His gun poked Rich in the hip with each jolt. They directed him to park in the valet area of the Sea View. With a nod of his weapon, the three exited the van and waited under the carport for a directive.

His partner disappeared into the hotel, yet every direction featured a similarly dressed fellow with the same tactical gear. The second soldier returned with two men, one sporting a black and blue mark on his cheek, the other dressed in a tuxedo jacket, and Bermuda shorts.

Tuxedo jacket spoke first, "Greetings, Mr. Malone. We have been waiting for your party." He turned to fire something in rapid Spanish to the other guy. When he only shrugged back, Tuxedo continued, "Is this your

complete party?"
Rich answered, "Huh?"
"Is this your complete party?" Another Spanish tirade. "Is this who you are traveling with?"
"What did you call me?"
"Mr. Malone. Is that not your name?" Tuxedo man snapped his fingers. Three more boys in black appeared from a side door. Guns directed on Rich. "Because if you are not—"
"No, I am. I thought you said something else."
"Wonderful," tuxedo man raised his hand. The boys shrunk back into the shadows. "I welcome you to the Seaview. Is this your entire party?"
Rich caught Ev and Celia's eyes, "Yes," he said.
"Okay. Good." He waited a minute before he continued, "And your friend…"
"My friend?"
"Yes, your friend. The other driver…"
"Phillippe?" Celia blurted out. Her hand flew to cover her mouth.
"Ah, mucho gracias senora. Yes – Phillippe,"
"He was some guy who offered us a ride at the church."
"What was at the church?"
"Clothes. Someone stole our things. We saw the church and went in. Phillippe offered us a ride."
"Ride to where?"

Rich shrugged his shoulders. "I don't know."
"You don't know?" A loud Spanish outburst followed. The circle of armed guards grew smaller, the longer the rant continued. Tuxedo man took a very long noisy inhale and stopped. "You don't know," he repeated.
"We were at the church, and Phillippe offered us a ride to the airport. We had seen a plane leave earlier and thought the airport might be back open." No one spoke. The tuxedo man started and stopped several times. He fell silent and walked back into the hotel lobby. The second soldier directed the group to a side door. They entered a large, empty ballroom and were hustled across through another door that leads directly into an elevator. On the eighth floor, they departed and walked to room 805. The soldier knocked twice and said, "Malone." The door opened to a suite overlooking the ocean. Two men sat at the breakfast bar. The rest of the room appeared empty. One stood and directed the threesome to the couch.
"You stay here," he instructed in broken English. "If you leave, we will kill you." All three walked out the door.
Ev turned towards her husband and asked, "How did they know our name?"
Rich shrugged to answer, "Damn if I know."
"Do you think?" Rich put his fingers to Ev's

lips.
"I try not to think."

Ric lay on one of the double beds snoring gently as only little boys can do. Maxi and Sam continued to stare at Sam's outline, adding and subtracting cards. The room had grown dark.
"Something isn't right," Sam said, his voice low. "They should be back. And where is Phillippe?"
"I thought the same thing yet..." Maxi gazed out on to the courtyard. Shadows passed by in silence. "Maybe one of us..."
"Yeah," Sam stood. "If I am not back in a half-hour, take Ric and head into the brush." Maxi nodded as Sam slipped out the door. She watched Ric sleep, his body moving in rhythm with his breath. The other sound, her heartbeat, brought little comfort.
Minutes moved slowly with each new noise bringing an increase of her pulse. When Sam opened the door, Maxi jumped up to a karate scan.

Maximum Trouble

"You do martial arts?" Sam asked. When Maxi shook her head no, he laughed. "Good to know. The situation is not pleasant." He handed over a brown paper bag. Inside sat two simple sandwiches and a box of juice. "This is all that is left. Apparently, we missed dinner. Phillippe and the rest never returned. Mayala, the office lady, said they would check it out once it got dark." He took half a sandwich out and bit into it. "She asked me to take the later watch shift, so I would be less obvious. Said she'd send someone to wake me in a few hours."

"Wake you?"

"She figures I'd sleep, I am not a psychic." He watched Maxi poking each layer of the sandwich. "For crying out loud, eat the damn thing," he barked. "We need a plan."

"I agree. When do you want to leave?"

"Like your style, kid. I think we need to at least try to rest. I am worried about my wife and your mom and dad. My instincts said we were semi-safe yet now..." he shrugs.

"Do you think we are safe here?"

"No. If we were, I'd be having a conversation with your dad, and we'd be eating something better than this," he holds up the sandwich. "I'll take first watch here, say give you a couple hours of shut-eye. Later you can switch off with me." Maxi nodded.

"What if I can't sleep?"

"Try…" Maxi lay next to Ric on the opposite bed. She watched Sam go between the slips of paper and the shadows on the window. She closed her eyes and brought her breath into a rhythm to drift away.

Maximum Trouble

Marjorie moved through Zack's office with the precision of a jeweler placing an exotic gem into a setting. She started with his desk, taking each item off the top to examine. His coffee mug, ashtray, and picture frame now lay smashed in the wastebasket by her feet.

All items from the top drawer: paperclips, stapler, pens, pencils, correction tape, red push pins separated from blue, an H.R. manual titled, *"Being Nice to Your Co-workers,"* and a pile of scrap paper, all containing a series of cartoon-like drawings.

"Not finding anything?" Spencer filled the doorway.

"Well, he obviously was sent the "be nice" book he obviously didn't read," Marjorie quipped back.

Spencer sat down on the leather couch against the wall. "What makes you think it's here?"

"I'm trying to think like Brady," that got an eye roll as a response. "He would take a copy with

him, yet he would keep a duplicate somewhere, just in case. We went through his townhouse from top to bottom. Even used the infrared yet came up with nothing." Marjorie slammed her hand down on the desk.
"Dammit, Spenc! It's here. I can feel it."
"Feel it? Really? You're starting to sound like Brady."
"Really. Think about it. Where would be the last place we'd look." Spencer shrugged.
"Here," Marjorie exclaimed as she swept her hands around the room. "Here," she repeated softer. "I am telling you what we need is here."
"I have a thought," Spencer leaned forward as if to rise. "What if Brady cleaned out his office ahead of leaving.'
"I'm his secretary. Don't you think I would know?"
"Marj, how would you know? He hardly talked to you."
"You have a point, Spencer. Working with Brady, I found him to be an in plain sight kind of guy. He'd leave classified memos on his desk."
"He did?" Marjorie pointed to the pile of papers. Spencer moved to the desk. Marjorie watched as he read a few lines of each. "These were lying around?"
"Yes. Which is why I think he didn't have enough time to stash it all. Think about what

we are looking for. A sheet of paper with names, perhaps? An analysis of a distribution map?" Marjorie moved around the desk to Spencer's side. "We were careful, yet Brady is observant. I don't think he had a lot."
"Why you say that?"
"Because if he did, we'd both be in jail. I want to find out if our friend had any inclination of our business dealings. That's all I care about."
Spencer moved towards the door. The sound of metal hitting glass filled the room.
"Drawer one is clean," Marjorie said as she smashed the wood against the floor.
"That's government property, right?"
"What can I say, the new guy refuses to use an old desk."

The AV-5 landed with a jolt, bumping up against the white sand shore. Zack watched the sniper crew collect its belongings and snap to attention as the door lowered for an exit. The small group disappeared into the dark. The only sound, the hum of their vehicle. The second team waited. Firearms ready if needed. They heard the engine stop and the quiet sounds of the island take over.

"Team one reporting," Zack heard in his earpiece. "Destination approximately 30 minutes. Team two in place." The soft movement of bodies heading down the ramp brought Zack's attention back to his task at hand. Team two ascended on to the soft sand. Off to the right, a brigade of footsteps moved towards the capitol. To his left, a line of men disappeared into the dark jungle.

He held back from the team long enough for the last person to disappear from the view of his naked eye. Armed with night vision, he could see their bodies move in between palm trees and blades of grass. Over his shoulder, Ken Boci stood. With a head nod, they both headed in a similar direction to team two yet off on their own path.

"The towers should be in view as soon as we cross the field," Ken whispered. Off to the side, a cluster of lights gave way to a small motel. Zack grabbed Ken's arm and pointed. Near a locked gate, the red glow of burning ash moved up and down. The distinct smell of marijuana floated by.

On the opposite side, another human became visible in the glow of the light. In the back of his shadow, the outline of a shotgun emerged. Zack watched as one spoke to the other in a Spanish dialect. He caught parts; Phillippe, van, Americans, yet could not make out the entire conversation.

Ken nodded to follow. "We need to travel to the towers," his voice somewhat audible.

The terrain of grass, roots, and rocks made the trek more of a challenge. The lights of the villages faded with the occasional unidentified wildlife scooting by their legs. The upward slope gave way to another view, this one with an outline of two towers in front, followed by dark everywhere else.

Zack gazed in the direction where the lights of the airport should be glowing. Team one should almost be in place. Below he could see team two heading in the course of the towers. He noted the time on his watch at the same time Ken did the same.

"Are we waiting for the fireworks," Ken asked.

"Not sure," Zack answered. "Something is off. My gut—"

"Oh, they told me you are one of those." Ken couldn't see Zack's return glare. "They told me about your gut." When no response took place, Ken continued, "Forget it. Let's do what we—" He took two steps and slipped on something substantial.

Zack jumped to shine a dim light on the area. A man's body lay next to another. Both had half their skull missing. Neither could be recognized as natives or tourists. Ken righted himself and examined the corpses.

"Two bodies, both shot. Dumped?" They moved the dim light around the area. In the short distance, the grass split and tire tracks led through the cavity. Something stood off to the side. "What's that?"

"Not sure." They walked the short distance to discover an old white building. The front doors nailed shut. Ken went to one side, while Zack did the same on the other. All entrances appeared to be secured tight. "Think it's worth breaking into?"

Zack kicked a hole in the small side door. The noise echoed. He reached inside and tried to wedge the wood open enough to enter. It gave way with a bang. "After you?" Zack indicated for Ken to go first.

"I don't think I'll fit," he gestured towards his bulk. Zack entered what appeared to be a small church. Wood benches lined up one behind the other, all faced towards a podium and cross. Cardboard boxes stacked across the border. Further examination exposed piles of t-shirts and shorts that had seen better days.

"Church," Zack said upon exiting. Back on the path, they watched explosions in the distance. Fire filled the skies. "Light show," he pointed in the direction. If team one had started their takeover of the airport, the time had become their number one enemy.

As the sky overhead filled with red explosions, the two pursued their quest towards the towers. Gunshots reverberated over the sand. Their movements quickened with each sound.

L.M. Pampuro

Ev stared out the balcony onto the beautiful turquoise ocean. The bright blue water sparkled. She brought her gaze down to the empty pool area. One man, holding a rifle, appeared to be appreciating the ocean view. She began to cry. Where are the children playing in the pool? Their imaginary giggles floated up through the air. What happened to the others? What would happen to them? Rich walked up and put his arms around his wife. "It will be okay," he said. His voice was soft enough for only her to hear.
"How do you know?"
"I don't." They stood in silence.
The hotel to the right appeared empty of life. No movement. On the left, people could be seen on balconies along with more soldiers and guns. Just past the left tower, the remains of a beachside villa sit in a pile of ash.
"Who was that guy in the tuxedo?" Celia

asked.

"I guess that is what we need to find out," Rich said. "It bothers me he knew my name."

Movement on the balcony next door had the group flinch. A young man walked out and gazed over the ocean. He turned, jumped, and settled. He brought his left hand over his mouth while pointing up with his right. All eyes lifted. In the corner of his balcony, a camera, red light flashing, recorded his every move. They turned to see the same flashing light on the edge of their balcony, recording theirs.

Maxi awoke to Sam entering the room. "Why didn't you wake me?" she said through yawns.
"I thought one of us needs to be alert during the day."
"But you needed sleep too."
"I got a few hours. That will be enough. Back in the city, I'd go days without sleeping while working a case. Haven't done that in a while, but I'll be alright."
Maxi nodded. "Any news?"
"Nada. Well, except there appeared to be an explosion and gunfire over by the airport. I could hear it while on the watch. Not sure what that means. Mayala is up in arms because of the Phillippe situation. They still haven't heard from him. Someone broke into the church last night, ripped the side door off." Sam made his way towards the bathroom. "I think that's about all for now."
Maxi sat wide-mouthed. Ric rolled over and, with one eye half-open, made his way into the

bathroom. He closed the door with a bang.
"Holy crap!" Maxi exclaimed.
"Yeah. And that is what I found out so far. I'm sure there's more." He turned back towards the closed bathroom door, "We need a freakin' phone charger." Sam moved to the opposite side of the room to stand in front of the wicker dresser. He opened each drawer, stared into its empty shell, and closed it. He repeated this action twice. "Wanted to make certain I didn't miss anything."

"What if we call from the room phone?" Maxi asked.

"Not a good idea. We don't know who we can trust…" He let the thought linger before adding, "You guys should eat breakfast. I'm going to sleep for an hour." Sam lay down in the space Ric had vacated. Within minutes his breathing became rhythmic.

Maxi scooted Ric outside the moment he emerged from the bathroom.

"Mom, where's grandma and papa?" his face turned into a worry scrunch.

"I'm not sure," Maxi answered. "We need to let Sam sleep and eat breakfast."

Outside the motel's office, Mayala had fruit and coffee set up. She handed each a plate and instructed to "Fill up." Ric spotted Cole, Gigi's son, across the way and brought his plate over to join him.

Out of earshot, Maxi inquired, "Do you have

any idea about where my parents are?"
To which Mayala responded, "No. Do you know where my son is?" Her eyes teared up though she showed no emotion otherwise.
"I'm sorry," Maxi choked. "We are both in pain." Mayala nodded. "May both of us find respectable news and peace."
"Amen."
Maxi joined Gigi and the boys off on a picnic table. "The amount of food is shrinking," Gigi noted. "This can't be good."
"Any word from your husband?" Maxi watched her shake her head. "My parents have disappeared too."
"That definitely isn't good," Gigi stood and motioned for her son to follow.
"Way to go, mom," Ric shoved a piece of melon in his mouth. He got up to go before Maxi had finished. "I'm going to head to the pool."
"Can you give me a minute?" Ric sighed. "Just go. And Ric, do not wake up, Sam." Maxi waved him off. She ate her fruit and watched Mayala jump at every noise. As she ate, she tried to visualize the notes Sam had strewed across the bed. The biggest challenge now is to find Celia and her parents. The second is to get off this freakin' island. Sam had heard gunshots coming from the direction of the airport.
That could be a positive thing.

Maximum Trouble

Simon had said they'd be safe here, but then again, his wife definitely had a fear of something or someone. Maxi stood and walked over to Mayala. "Is there a working phone I could use?"

Mayala walked around the side of the building. She turned to make the same move in the opposite direction. "I have a phone, but..." She waved Maxi inside. "If they find out..."

"Who is they?"

"I can't tell you. Can you call your father?"

"I can try, but his phone is probably dead." Mayala made the sign of the cross. "I was going to try my brother...if I can remember his number. I definitely remember his email."

"Email..." Mayala waved for Maxi to follow her into the cold, dark office. The empty room led around the counter into an adjacent area. The second room had seen better days. What was once ocean blue walls now appeared a dingy blue-gray. A small desk with a dated monitor is positioned within view of the doorway. Off on the side, a queen bed in need of being made up sits next to a counter, stove, and refrigerator can be seen on the other side.

Mayala gestured for Maxi to sit. "I will watch the door," she instructs. "You have five minutes."

"Let's hope Pete is online and able to email me back." Maxi sat and logged into her email.

"Only one hundred and seven," she commented.
"What?" Mayala poked her head in.
"Nothing... talking to myself." She searched to find no new correspondence from Pete or Zack. She typed *Mom And Dad Have Disappeared* in the subject line and clicks to the body area. *Mom and Dad went to a church to get clothes with their friend and have been gone since yesterday. The lady who runs the Paradise Motel, where me, Ric, and our friend Sam are, sent her son out with them. He, along with Sam's wife, is missing too. My spidey sense (stop laughing) tells me this is bad. There were explosions last night over by the airport. My phone is dead. Not sure when I'll be back online...Any information is appreciated."
Maxi hit send. She read the subject lines as she started to delete non-essential correspondence. As her finger lingered above the delete button, most of the emails fell under non-essential as they disappear from view. She sat back to watch the screen. Nothing. Her attention expanded to volleying between Mayala and the screen.
Still nothing.
Mayala poked her head back in, Maxi shrugged and logged out. "Come back in a couple hours, and we can check again."
Back at the room, Ric lay on one bed reading

a borrowed comic book while Sam snored a symphony on the other. Maxi took out the notes to again stare at the pile

"There has got to be something here," she stared.

Movement out by the pool caught her eye. She glanced up to see the tall dreadlocked man from the hotel business center standing at the edge of the pool. She opened the slider curtains a tad further to peek at what had his attention. At the same moment, he turned back in the direction of her room.

Her stomach broke out in a Grateful Dead drum solo, producing a layer of sweat all over her body. She tried to peek out the small crack, only to find the man had moved out of view. The peephole in the door proved useless too. Sam's snores could be heard echoing throughout the room.

When Ric opened his mouth to comment, Maxi "shushed" him from across the way. For once, he didn't argue. A loud bang came from the backside. Maxi crossed the room again, try and peek to see what happened. She watched as Gigi and Cole disappeared into Mayala's office.

A minute later, Mayala took her seat in front. The man came back and waved a pistol as he spoke.

"Where is the wife?" he bellowed.

"I don't know. They go. Phillippe go. Everybody

go!" she shouted back.

"Listen, woman," he pointed the gun at her face, "if I found out you are lying—"

"Talin, you listen. I am an old woman. I have no reason to lie to you or anyone else. My son is missing. When the airport closed my guest, they leave. You can go check. There is only family staying here because there is no work. All the tourists are gone. Very bad for business..." in a very piercing voice, she added, "And my son is gone. I have nothing." Mayala spits on the ground next to his foot. The man stepped back. "Mayala, I should kill you right now," he shouted. By this time, Sam had woken up and stood behind Maxi. He observed the exchange yet said nothing. The man continued to scream in half Spanish and half something they couldn't make out.

Mayala sat and said nothing. "I will be back," he stated and walked off towards the gate. A car engine revved as tires squealed. Maxi and Sam waited a few minutes before sprinting to the office.

"Stay put," she instructed Ric. In the office, Gigi sat in the corner, crying and apologizing. At the same time, Mayala held her on one side and Cole on the other. Both Maxi and Sam stood in the doorway. Mayala gestured for both to enter.

"This is all my fault!" Gigi wailed. They

watched Mayala for a clue. "If my husband hadn't gone back for his stupid computer, they never would have found us." She met Maxi's eyes, "And your parents would all be fine." Gigi placed her arm around Mayala, "And your son," she cried. The rest of the rant went from a mix of swear words bracketed by her husband's name and uncontrollable fits of sobbing.

"This will be okay," Mayala whispered. She rubbed both backs as she spoke. "Everything will be alright..."

Zack's approached the towers with caution. He looked around for any sign of team two, yet no indications of their presence could be found. Ken stood to his left and waited.
"Where did they go?" he asked. His eyes are scanning the horizon.
"I don't know. There haven't been any communications."
"The tower on the right is heavily guarded," Ken pointed to movement off the balconies, "Yet the left side appears clear." Zack nodded. With his goggles, he could make out the snipers on the lower floors. He again scanned the area with no sight of his team.
"We should scan the perimeter and head to the left," he points.
"Should we try to communicate with the team?"
Zack shakes his head no. "Less communication is better at this point." The desert climate made hiding difficult yet

walking amongst the scraps of grass and cactus, along with the sun rising, made shielding their presence a little easier.

Their path had roots and stumbling blocks, yet as they ascended a small hill, an abandoned strip mall came into view. They moved with caution towards the front. The one-story building contained a liquor store; shelves and coolers empty of product, along with a convenience store, and tiny restaurant. No sound emerged.

Ken peered inside the restaurant, only to be pulled backward. "What the—!" he exclaimed as a hand clasped over his mouth. He bit hard into the chubby fingers as an elbow slammed into his side. Falling backward, Ken caught sight of Rod holding his hand.

"Asshole," both whispered in unison.

Zack walked in with his gun drawn. He holstered it after accessing the situation. "What's the status?"

"I'm waiting here for the transports. Our guys moved about thirty people through. Didn't you hear the jeeps?" Both Zack and Ken confessed they hadn't. "Good. We started to clear the tower on the left-right after the fireworks started. So far, no resistance."

"Anyone on the other side?" Ken stood off to the side.

"Whoever is there is under heavy guard. I called it earlier. I think our intelligence is off."

"Why is that?" Zack waited.

"Because moving these people has been easy, too easy. Whoever is behind this, and I think they are here not at the airport—"

"Why is that?"

"Did you notice the guards on the right?" Both Zack and Ken nodded. "They have to be searching for someone specific because at a couple points we were in range—"

"And they didn't engage."

"Which is questionable. We also believe people are being held in the right tower too." Zack and Ken waited for Rod to continue. Something out front drew his attention from the conversation. A red, gold, and green painted bus with the letters *Island Party* pulled up by the door. Rod held up one finger and went out to meet it. He returned moments later with two men, both in their twenties and a second gun, as the bus pulled away, heading back towards the AV-5.

"These gentlemen were not invited to the party," he exclaimed. "Why were you on the bus?" When either spoke, he hit one in the side of the head with the gun he had confiscated. He waited. "I'm going to ask one more time and first your friend, and then you join the pile of bodies in the scrub."

When neither spoke again, Rod cocked his arm back only to stop with Ken's yell. "Let me try something," Ken suggested, in perfect Spanish, he asked why they were on the bus. The two exchanged quick glances. The one holding on to the side of his head answered in his own language. "Huh," Ken said. "The boy here says they were offered safe passage for their families if they got on the American bus and shot whoever picked them up."

"Safe passage for who?" Zack asked. Ken repeated the question and listened.

"For his mother and brothers. They already killed his uncle for helping the Americans."

In perfect Spanish, Zack asked who is in charge? "Am I the only one here who took French in high school?" Rod joked. They waited as the boys debated in whispers about what to say. One pointed to his head while the other, wide-eyed, said something about their mother.

In broken English, the non-injured one answered, "We do not know. These people came in a big boat three days ago. They were seeking three families on the island. They didn't say why. We were told to either help or go on the boat." The other kid added to this. "My cousin said they loaded up the boat and blew it up. After we became afraid."

"Who is doing all this?" Zack repeated.

"The man in the tuxedo," the kid whispered. "There is another man too. He is an island person, but he is not an island person. He is horrible!"

"A man in a tuxedo and an island person," Ken through his hands up. "And we still have no motive."

"Do you remember the names of the people they were looking for?" Zack asked.

The kid glanced down at his cousin's injury. "No names," he answered.

Zack held up a twenty-dollar bill. "Are you sure you do not hear any names?"

The boys stared at the money. They spoke in silence before answering, "Jacobs, Malone, and Atwood."

"Shit," Zack exclaimed.

Maximum Trouble

Sam stood off to the side. He watched the exchange with Mayala then walked away. Maxi found him smoking a cigarette leaning against a palm tree, staring in the direction the van disappeared in long ago. He didn't move as she approached.

"Sam, we can't stay here," Maxi's voice rose above a whisper. "We are putting Mayala's family in too much danger." Sam took a long inhale. He let the smoke curl out his nose. He inhaled another deep breath. "Sam?"

"Yeah," he blew a sigh.

"Yeah?" Sam turned to Maxi. She noted his expression remained neutral, he wore his cop face.

"I agree we need to move to get Mayala out of danger. Believe it or not, I am thinking, Maxi. Not everyone thinks out loud." Maxi's complexion turned a darker shade of red than her current sunburnt stage. Her pulse quickened. She turned to walk back towards the room. "Maxi," Sam's voice stopped her,

"Look, I need to come up with a plan. We can't just leave."

She nodded as her shoulders slumped. "You are right," she murmured. "What's—" she stopped midsentence. Sam glared back at her. Ric's voice carried as splash noises echoed over the wall. Maxi moved in his direction. Sam followed.

"We can't leave Gigi here," he stated. Maxi nodded. "The more of us there are, the harder it is for us to hide." He looked back at the wall. "We need to find Celia and your mom and dad too." The mention of her parents sent a shiver.

"I have a feeling—"

"Ya, me too. Yet I think they are okay for now." Maxi nodded. "The island is small. That is the problem. I'm thinking if we go by vehicle, we'll get caught. Yet walking, where should we go?"

"We are stuck?"

"No. There is always a solution." He walked back towards the courtyard. "I need to review my notes. Either way, we are leaving after dinner."

"Should I talk to Mayala?"

"No. The less she is aware of, the better. Find Ric and pack up. Fill the water bottles and grab fruit, if you can do it without raising suspicions. Got it?" Maxi nodded. "I am going to find a place. And then we find the rest of our party."

Maxi followed Sam part way to the room. She broke off to sit in one of the lounge chairs. Ric stood within her view, along with Gigi and two others, which she did not recognize. She watched Gigi's animated gestures. One of the men watched every move she made while the other glanced around the pool area. He moved in Maxi's direction. Maxi moved her feet closer to her body to remain out of sight by the grace of an abundant seagrass bush.

She watched the exchange a little longer. As quiet as possible, she pulled herself up off the chair. The slapping sound of her flesh escaping from the plastic chair filled the air. Maxi tiptoed in the direction of the room, avoiding the visible sightlines.

Sam had a map of Aruba along with his notes scattered around the edge arranged on one of the beds. He stood over the collage of paper and stared. He did not move when Maxi entered. She stood behind him.

A red pen outlined the airport and hotel row. Another set of circles highlighted Madame Janette's, Mayala's place, and LaCabana. All the highlighted areas made a path dividing the island in half. To the north, an uninhabited area around where The Natural Bridge once stood. Both knew there was nothing there but desert.

To the east lay a few smaller towns mostly

inhabited by commercial fishermen and families who lived on the island for generations. To the west, more small villages. Maxi pointed to the villages in the west, noting her once-perfect manicure, now chips of blue polish and slivers of the nail, contrasted with the light blue background.

"What about here?" Sam followed her finger to the spot on the map.

"Why there?"

"Fewer people? Maybe the assholes who are doing this wouldn't bother there?"

"You sound like your mother," Sam noted. Maxi's eyes started to water. "Don't worry," he gave her an awkward hug, "my Celia wouldn't let me off this easy in life, and as long as your parents are with Celia, they are all safe."

"Now you sound like my dad," Maxi guffawed. She wiped the tears from her cheek before she added, "What's our plan?"

"Great minds think alike. Over here," he pointed at a small village on the north coast, "seems like the most likely choice..."

"But?"

"But it is a problem. If we go there and it isn't safe—"

"We are stuck."

"Exactly."

"And we can't ask Mayala," Sam shook his head no, "so we go with our gut." Maxi waited

while Sam stared at the map again. "We can't be in a standstill. I vote, yes."
"We leave at dusk," Sam said.
"Just like in a bad movie."
"If only..." Maxi looked out the sliders. "Should I talk to Gigi, or should you?"
"I have been thinking about that. Do you recognize who those two guys are?" Maxi shook her head no. "Yeah, me neither. They haven't been at any meals and suddenly appear after the goon squad."
"You don't think..."
"I'm not sure. I'd like to wait until after dinner to talk with Gigi, just in case."

Dinner consisted of zucchini, local squash, and onion served along with some type of fish. Mayala brought out two mangos cut up as a dessert for all to share. Maxi noted the shrinking portions. "You take the first watch," Mayala instructed Sam, who nodded back in her direction.
Gigi sat off to the side of the group with her kid. When they got up to leave, Sam and Maxi followed. "Gigi, we need to talk to you." She instructed Cole to go back to the room. Maxi watched Ric follow.
"I know what you are going to say. If Walter..." Sam held up his hand to stop her. "That's not what we need to talk to you about." He guided her by the elbow back to their room. Ric sat

on the opposite bed, next to two stuffed backpacks. "Ric, would you go visit Gigi's kid, please?" Maxi moved her head in the direction of the door. She watched him sulk out and look back at the last minute, meeting her gaze. She gave a soft smile back.

After he left, Sam pointed to the map. "Look, Gigi, we can't stay here. We are putting Mayala and her family in extreme danger." Gigi opened her mouth to speak, yet Sam continued before she could, "This is not anyone's fault. It just is." He moved the map for a better view. "The red circles are places we have been along with areas we believe we should avoid." She nodded. "The other areas are places we are not sure of, yet we believe they are safe."

"What do you mean, believe are safe? We aren't safe here?"

"It doesn't matter if we are safe here. Our presence is putting some decent people in danger," Maxi said.

"We are leaving in a half-hour and would like you to come with us. Our plan is to move in this direction," Maxi noted Sam pointed towards the east where the fishing villages lay. "We think once there, we may be able to contact someone for help."

"What about Walter? How will he find us?" Maxi and Sam exchanged glances. "We got to

tell someone where we are going otherwise..."
"Gigi, we can't. It is for our safety." She nodded and moved towards the door.
"Let me think," she said.
"Not for too long," Maxi warned. They watched her walk out the door. After a few minutes, Maxi spoke, "You pointed in the opposite direction."
"Just in case." Sam folded his makeshift map small enough to fit in his pocket. "We should be ready to leave, with or without her." Maxi nodded.

Commander Atwood sat back in his office, a half-eaten turkey sandwich on the far corner of his desk with a glass of iced green tea in grabbing distance of his hand. He watched the explosion at the Aruba airport on his satellite monitor as he scribbled notes on the legal pad to his right.

Pete Malone sat off to the side on a black leather couch, watching the same activity on his laptop. "Something is off," he noted.

"You feel it too?" The commander leaned back in his chair. "Our guys got to the airport—

"Bad intelligence—

"There seems to be no fight—

Pete stared at his computer screen. "If the airport is destroyed—"

"There are fewer ways for people to arrive on and off the island. I thought of that too."

Atwood took a sip of tea. "I think we did their dirty work for them. That was too easy for us."

"How do you think we were compromised?"

"From the ground, possibly."

"That makes perfect sense. Now we need to figure out if this is someone on our team or if our satellite is compromised." Pete re-typed a few keystrokes. He scanned a transcript of one of the prisoners from the West coast. He pointed towards the text. "I hate to bring this up, but do you think that Russia is involved?"

"What made you consider Russia?"

"Look," Pete pointed at the transcript. "it says here that the sailor had a tattoo on his right arm of a skull with a crown smoking a cigar—"

"Russian Navy?"

"Or a hired gun. I would like to request a visual, sir." Hit send before the response of "By all means," left the Commander's mouth. He sat back in his chair. Silence filled the room.

"When did the activity start to shift? Can we pinpoint the moment it picked up?" The commander sat up. "Pete, where is your father's cell phone signal coming from now?" Pete opened a new tab, typed in a few keystrokes. A map of Aruba came onto his screen. He leaned on the zoom button until he had a street-level view.

"The signal is still at The Seaview Resort."

"Can we see a visual?" He switched back to his first screen, typed in code as the commander moved to sit next to him. A grainy photo appeared. Both leaned forward. "Look at that," Pete pointed towards the tower on the left. The lens automatically zoomed in on several people dressed in black carrying guns along the roof. Using his mouse, he did a full circle of the area.

"Look here," he pointed down to the street level where several black Humvees were parked in the valet area. "Those are not our vehicles." He moved the screen view to the tower on the right. There stood what appeared to be an empty high rise.

"Can we move closer to the second building?" Pete moved around his mouse while he punched in additional number/letter combinations. "Wait, what is that?" They moved the camera to focus on a red beam emulating from one of the floors.

"I can't tell from here, and the camera is stuck."

"Stuck? The U.S. freakin' military spends billions on this shit, and it gets stuck?" The commander rose up to stretch. He started to pace across his office. He took in deep breaths and released each to the rhythm of his movements. Pete counted ten steps across. The commander stopped on the seventh, "Are you thinking what I am?"

"That we got hosed by this vendor?" The commander narrowed his eyes." Pete sat up a bit straighter. "I am not sure what direction

you are going in, sir."
"I am thinking we have been set up." In two steps, the commander had his phone in hand. "I need a list of who logged onto the Aruba situation." Pete watched his face turn a shade of red. "This is stat, Sargent, not a request." He listened a few more minutes while Pete continued to punch in various codes. "I wanted the information five minutes ago." He slammed the phone back on its cradle while mumbling something Pete could not understand. "Malone," the commander shouted. "We need to reassemble the team here and via satellite in five." Pete turned to ask a question, yet all he saw was the commander's back leaving the room.

A beep indicated an email. Pete hit the file. "I'll be damned." The tattoo matched the description. He hurried after the Commander.

Zack watched Boci stop his inquisition and grab his phone. "Heads up," he shouted as the phone flew across the room in his direction. He caught the object mid-air and stared at the screen. "This is why you need my clearance," Boci boasted as he continued to ask questions in perfect island dialect.

The readout said a meeting in five, yet the phone screen blurred between the readable announcement and an icon of an orange cartoon duck winking. Zack pounded the screen with his index finger trying in vain to refresh. He turned away from the crowd as vibration from his pocket had his body shield the action of pulling the phone out.

Crystal clear on his screen the words *Meeting in two. Secure channel six* appeared. He glanced back at Boci's screen. The winking duck stared back. Zack pressed the attend button on his phone and waited for the all-clear.

Maximum Trouble

"Yo, Brady, what's up with my line?" Zack turned as Ken approached.

"Duck issues," he answered as he threw the device back.

"What the hell?" The violent tapping of Ken's index finger echoed. "Son of a..." Zack watched Ken walk outside. He turned his back towards the group, all of which continued to watch Ken's rant, walking and swearing as he held his phone in different directions.

Zack connected an earpiece. He turned back in the direction of the others yet held his phone out of view. Pete's voice came through the static.

"Zack, press the zip if you could hear me." Zack leaned away to press in the numbers 037. He waited. "He's in," Pete's voice came through. "Are you in a place to speak?" Zack pressed 2. "Crap."

"My sentiments exactly," he mumbled. The two boys from the bus watched as Zack turned away.

"Here is what we know," Zack listened, his face neutral. He glanced out the window. Ken stood outside the bus, still yelling into his phone. "Seaview... Heavily guarded... Distraction... Airport... Plant..." Every third word came through clear, the rest gibberish. "Do you understand?" Zack pressed 3. The line went dead.

The two boys from the bus sat at an

abandoned red Formica table in the corner. The others had moved outside. Zack watched their attention shift from Ken's rant to the high rises along the beach. Ken barreled back in, red-faced.

"This Japanese garbage phone allowed me to hear almost nothing of the briefing!" His arm cocked back, Ken threw the phone with force. Those within ranged jumped as it shattered against the concrete wall. "I couldn't hear a goddamn thing!"

A soft breeze entered the building, yet no one moved in the silence. A distant call from a seagull echoed in the distance.

"Feel better?" Zack picked up a shard piece of plastic and tossed it in the wastebasket next to Ken.

"No." Ken's breathing started to slow. "But I am getting there." He turned back towards Zack, "Any thoughts?"

"A few," Zack muttered. "What information exists about the hotel over there?" He chin nodded in the direction of The Seaview.

"Nothing really. It is heavily guarded, but you can see it." Zack nodded. "I bet you these folks know a thing or two." Rod came back in from the parking lot. He produced a long knife from his pocket. The two natives at the table began speaking rapid Spanish at the same time Rod lunged in their direction.

"Stop," Zack commanded. The room went still. "Puede decirme sobre el hotel de allí?" (Can you tell me about the hotel over there?) The two looked at Zack, each other, and over to Rod. Their eyes widened. "Por favor..." (Please).

"Te dijimos que hay un hombre loco ..." (We told you he is a crazy man).
"Dime mas." (Tell me more). Zack watched the two. One opened his mouth while the other nodded no. Hands flew up and down.

"Mi hermano y yo, (My brother and I) e tienen miedo al loco Vivimos en paz en esta isla y luego ... (are afraid of the crazy man. We lived in peace on this island...)"
"Who is this crazy man?" Zack asked in perfect Spanish.
"Se ve como un rasta, pero no hay nada pacífico en él. No sé su nombre." (He looks like a rasta but there is nothing peaceful about him. Please do not ask his name.)
"Grazie."
"So, what is the deal?" Rod's voice boomed from behind Zack. Ken hovered close by.
"They say there is a crazy rasta in charge. That is all they know."
"What are you thinking? Recon?" Zack didn't answer. Instead, he walked out of the building to gaze at The Seaview. Both Ken and Rod followed. "Yo, Brady?"
Zack held up one finger. He walked back into

the room. "We need to figure out what information we have," he started to say, "then we can assume what we don't."

"In other words, we need a plan," Rod caught Ken's attention with a silent glance. Both nodded.

Maximum Trouble

The seagrass grew as thick as fog taking visibility down to what appeared in front of the group. "Eek"
"Another bug?"
"Sorry." The only exchange of words. Sam stopped to look up into the star-speckled sky.
"Hear that?" his voice so low Maxi could almost hear, yet Ric needed to come closer.
"That's what I mean. It is quiet. Almost too quiet."
"What do you mean?" Ric questioned.
"Sometimes, silence isn't a good thing." Ric nodded as if he understood.
"Are we going to where Papa and Gram are?" Maxi reached around to hug her only child.
"Fingers crossed," Sam said. He pushed more reeds aside to continue. "By my read, we should be in a town in another twenty minutes." Maxi nodded, yet she knew neither could see. With Sam leading, Ric in the middle, and Maxi swatting flies and jumping at every sound from behind, the group continued their conquest in silence.

Marjorie could hear Spencer swearing from down the hall. She eased the door open to Zack's old office for a full view. She could only see Spencer's back along with papers flying over the desk, skimming to a stop along the carpet.

"Lose something?" Marjorie asked at the same time, placing a ceramic UConn mug on the desk. She sipped from the cup in her opposite hand.

"It really is not here." Spencer sat up. He spilled a couple drops of the brown liquid as he grabbed the mug to take a drink. He stopped right before his mouth. "You don't think he took it, do you?"

"You keep asking me the same question. All I can say hon is that Zack Brady is one sharp cookie."

"So, you keep telling me." He watched Marjorie raise her cup to her lips, tilt it back, and snort down another gulp.

Maximum Trouble

"Look Spec," he winced, "I'm saying Zack was smart. That's all. Other than that observation, I found him to be a condescending pain in the ass."

"That makes two of us." He jiggled the middle drawer. "I mean, who puts a lock on a middle desk drawer? Top drawer, I understand. The bottom drawer makes sense. But in the middle?"

"I say we bust it open."

"Marjorie, if this was anyone else's desk, I would say the same. But—

"It might be boobytrapped—

"Knowing Zack—

"So, we need to be careful." Spencer moved from behind the desk, leaning off the front. "We can call the bomb squad to open it."

"Spencer, darling. That would attract attention, no? We can figure this out or find someone to open it we trust, but don't like." Marjorie's laugh gave Spencer chills. He never could figure out when she was serious.

Getting the subject back on track, Spencer refocused the conversation, "Did you find anything interesting on the laptop?"

"Just the usual shit from our department. Are we sure he didn't have two?"

"I sent a couple of our guys over to his place. Nothing interesting except a few security cameras."

Marjorie reached to take Spencer's now empty mug. "Why would he need security cameras?"
"That's my question."   Spencer picked up a random piece of paper. He muttered the subject line, "Group meeting for Shadow agenda," he crumpled it into a ball. He tossed the page into a pile next to the wastebasket. Marjorie watched as he repeated the action. Not one page making it into the receptacle.
"Spencer, you don't think he stilled worked in intelligence, and our place was a—
"Rouse? Could be. Although I thought we were off the radar, that is until our friend decided to blow up a cruise ship full of Americans." Spencer started to pace. "I mean, who does that?"
"Crazy people."
"No, shit." He leaned over for a view out the open door. A few people milled about down the hall. The new day's activity on the verge of a start. "Marjorie, tell me again how we got into this?"
"I can give you a billion reasons once we own Aruba."
"No, seriously. The bureau tracks this stuff." She did a full eye-roll at Spencer. "Large amounts of cash, sudden new cars, lavish vacations. They keep tabs on everything—"
"If they knew everything, we would be in a penitentiary right now, probably in God-

forsaken Florida or some other crazy place." She walked around the desk to drape her arms around Spencer's shoulders. "This is all going to work out," she brought his chin up to meet her gaze. "Trust me, love. I know what I am doing."

Spencer tilted his head to rest on her shoulders. "Sure, expect so," his voice barely audible, "I sure look forward to…"

Maxi slapped a green fly off of Ric's back. "Thanks, mom," he muttered. She watched her son shuffled in front of her. The only indication of Sam leading the way was the movement of the grass ahead. The foliage had begun to thin, and the group could see some sort of light in the distance. Soon they would have no cover.

Maxi prayed for clouds to take out the moon's beacon.

"What is that?" Ric whispered. "It smells like barbequed chicken." His stomach let out a growl.

"I smell food, too," Maxi added. Sam shushed the two.

"Stay here and do not move," he instructed. "I am going to see what's what." Maxi nodded. She rested her arm around Ric's chest. Within minutes, voices carried above the weeds, followed by the sounds of rustling grass.

Maxi held Ric tighter.

Maximum Trouble

"There have to be others," a man's voice with a prominent island accent proclaimed. "Find them."

Maxi and Ric stood still. Grass moved ten feet to their right. "Mom…" Maxi cupped her hand over Ric's mouth while shaking her head no.

The movement came closer. Both crouched down low in the grass. Maxi shielding Ric with her body. "I don't see anyone," the voice stood a few feet in front of where they hid.

A shout from behind, followed, "Neither do I."

"No one over here," came from about twenty feet away. Maxi held her breath. Ric's heart pounded against her hands. "I'm going in."

"Ya, man, me, too." A sharp piece of something scraps against Maxi's arm. "Don't want the barbeque gone like last night." His laugh felt against their bodies. Both frozen in the grass.

"I am coming too," another voice echoed off their backs. The grass swayed around their bodies. When the long stalks stop, Maxi rises. Not ten feet away a man stands, lenses reflect the little light in the sky as they scan the reeds. His movements methodical, deliberate, he turns the glow in her direction. The perfect circles parallel, shine.

"Yo, mon. Don't make me run. We already have your friend." Maxi feels Ric's small body by her side, statuesque.

"What, mon. Are you seeing things again?" He turns in the direction of the voice at the same moment both Maxi and Ric disappear into the grass.

"Must be," they hear. "I thought if I asked for whoever is with that dude to come forth, they would." Laughter echoes. "for our splendid food and company."

"Mon, the universe doesn't work that way." The man continues to scan over the reeds.

"Mine does." Maxi shutters in the silence. "What are we doing with him?"

"Bring him to Talin?"

"Then, he is dead." Maxi moved her hands to cover Ric's ears. He sat still. "You can see he is American."

"Should we give the man a death sentence because of his home?" The smell of skunk waffled thru the air.

"Choices, my friend. Him or us." More movement in the opposite direction. Maxi let out a breath.

"Mom?" Ric whispered. She shushed him. The two sat as silence rolled in. Ric turned around in Maxi's arms. Their faces lined up. "Mom," he whispered again. Maxi winced. The kid needed a toothbrush. "What are we going to do?"

"I don't know."

Maximum Trouble

"We can't let them kill Sam," he squeaked. Maxi kissed his wet cheek.

"No, we can't."

"We need a plan." Ric sat back on the ground. A shadow moved behind his mother. Maxi jumped at the touch of a hand on her back. A figure about Ric's height shushed the two as he pulled Maxi back into the reeds.

She slapped his hand away. "Please follow me," a boy's voice pleaded. "Those are not nice people."

Ric leaned over his mother, "I'm Ric," he introduced and stuck his hand out.

"I am Bob. My family calls me Moon." The two boys shook hands.

"Why?"

"Because I like to be out at night," Moon laughed. His hand slapped over his mouth. "Shush." He waited. A cool breeze wiggled the reeds. "We have to go." Moon jumped up and spun around. He pointed to the left.

"We can't leave our friend," Ric said.

"Where is your friend?" Rick pointed in the direction Sam had disappeared. The boy shook his head no as he spoke, "You have to for now. It is not safe here."

"Mom, what do we do?" Maxi watched at both boys. Her stomach growled yet remained calm. There were no flip flops. She looked in the direction Sam had disappeared.

"We can't leave our friend," she repeated.

"Whoosh," Moon blew out a breath. "You really can't stay here. Come with me and talk to my mother. She will understand how to find your friend."

Before Maxi could comment, Ric said, "Do you have food?"

"Not a lot, but we can share." Moon's body jerked between sitting and next to Ric and jumping up to peer in the same direction as Maxi.

"Let's go, mom," Ric started to walk in Moon's direction.

"Now wait a minute—

"We don't have a choice." Maxi knew he was right yet still held back.

"Fine." Ric wiggled out his hand. Maxi thrust hers out to remake the connection. "Lead on."

Maximum Trouble

In the small conference room, Pete and Commander Atwood sat and stared at the satellite image projected on the screen. A grainy picture of Pete's parents appeared on the balcony of The Seaview. Smoke billowing from their lips. A few floors above the two, a man in black sat with a machine gun resting on his lap. In the next tower, Commander Atwood's son, Walter, appeared on another balcony.

"As usual, they found a place to smoke," Pete observed.

"Excuse me?"

"Sorry, Commander, it is frustrating my parents could be in real danger, yet they would worry more about finding a place to smoke a cigarette than their situation."

"Pete, I hate to tell you this, but smoking could be their coping mechanism." Pete started to roll his eyes, then stopped. He turned towards his commanding officer and cleared his throat.

"There are cameras all over this place," Pete noted. He took an electronic highlighter to make circles around several areas. "Also, there are six guards stationed in various places." Again, he highlighted the placement.

"There hasn't been any movement of people from either building, correct?"

"Only those who our boys have extricated." Pete nodded.

"Do you think the captures are aware of who they have?"

Pete again nodded no. "My gut tells me no because if they did, especially with Walter, I am confident we would have heard."

"Agreed." The Commander stared at the image. "Have we heard from Brady and company?"

"Not recently. As far as we can tell, the concentration is on moving people out. So far, the transport made six runs. We have one crew watching the tower and another moving people."

"What about the other?"

"Out of communication at this time." Atwood nodded. Pete went back to switching his attention between screens.

"Anything on the rest of the island?"

"Pretty quiet so far, sir." Pete waited for a beat before adding, "Any news on the Russia connection as yet?"

Maximum Trouble

Commander Atwood hushed him. "Do you want to start World War Three?" he barked back. A deep wheezy breath later, he said, "Pete, do you still have that old connection?" Pete nodded. "Off the record—"

"Off the record can get us both court marshaled, sir." Atwood blew out another breath, this one louder than the last. He stared down at his next in command. Pete shifted in his chair before volunteering that he could make a query. He typed a quick note, hesitated over the keys before he hit send. "And they are still trying to track who logged on to our secured site besides those with authority."

"One would think—"

"Yes, one would." Pete changed screens on his laptop. "Well, I'll be damned." The commander looked over his protégé's shoulder to follow Pete's finger. "Maxi is okay, or at least she was." He read the email aloud.

"Send team A over there and obtain a report on the damn airport situation!" Atwood closed his eyes. "And Pete, let me know when you hear from our friend."

"Yes, sir!" Pete saluted. "We should have news in that area soon."

"Old news, yet good news, son."

Through the grass, Moon leads the two to a clay hut surrounded by palm trees. The ocean waves slapped in the distance. A small woman in cut off shorts and a dancing bear t-shirt poked at the ambers of a glowing fire. Her blonde dreadlocks tied back with a purple ribbon. Her focus did not waver as Moon sat at her side.

"What did you find this time, my moony?"

"The bad men were trying to find them," he pointed in the direction of Maxi and Ric. His mother didn't move. "They needed our help." The older woman nodded. "You said no more, but mama..."

She glanced in Maxi's direction, her eyes reflecting the fire that started to grow. "Moony, we must be careful. Your father---

"Is an ass—

"Moony. We must have some respect."

"But if father hadn't met the—

Maximum Trouble

"Shush!" Moon's mother rose from behind the fire. She walked over and extended her slim hand. Maxi jumped. Her hand tingled with the touch. "I am Harmony, Moon's mother."

"Maxi," head nods towards Ric, "Ric's mother." Both women gave a quick nod.

"How did you find us?" Harmony asked. Her eyes are not wavering from Maxi's.

"We didn't. Your son found us. The boys decided coming here is our best bet."

"Best bet?" She watched Maxi open her mouth to speak before closing it again. "But you are unsure."

"Honestly, Harmony, I am not certain of anything." Maxi started to explain their predicament when Harmony held her hand up.

"Doesn't matter," she interrupted. "You can't stay here. We can give you food—"

"Mom!"

"Moony, it is too dangerous." Harmony brought her focus back to Maxi. "We can feed both of you and give shelter to stay the night." She listened for a moment before lowering her voice, "I can see about your friend. Yet in the morning, you must leave." Harmony brought her voice down lower, "For your safety as well as ours."

Maxi nodded. "I understand. We've had some great folks help us. If I could find a phone charger or a computer with the internet, I could communicate with my brother."

"My uncle works in D.C," Ric stated. Maxi broke eye contact with Harmony to glare at her son.

"D.C., huh?" Harmony repeated.

"It is not a big deal. He works there," Harmony nodded

"Let's get you two into our village. For tonight," Harmony repeated, "you will sleep in our tent. In the meantime, I want to give you something to eat." She disappeared down a path alongside the hut. Moony pulled Ric in the direction his mother had headed.

"Wait!" Maxi said a bit too loud. Moony shushed her. "Just give me a minute."

"Mom, I'm hungry." Maxi held up one finger. "That is her thinking pose," Ric said as he rolled his eyes.

"Ric's mom, if I may," Moony interrupted. He took Maxi's hand in his. "My father is a bad man, but my mother is a respectable woman. She will help you as best she can." Maxi nodded. "Please come with us, at least until sunrise. It is dangerous for you to be out, especially as Americans."

Maxi stared at the path, now illuminated by the glow of the fire. She looked back at the field they had navigated through. She found neither direction appealing. Her hand found

her stomach. She waited. When no nausea crawled to her throat, she released her hands to her side.
She took Ric's hand in hers. "Okay, we'll follow you." Moony lead the way, Ric in the middle, while Maxi followed, peering over her shoulder, trying to memorize the way back.

Ken Boci paced outside the abandoned restaurant vexing between speaking and holding his hands up to the star-studded sky. Zack sat with his back to the building. He despised the waiting as much yet learned to control and conserve his energy long ago.

The rescue team cleared the first building at dusk. The Seaview held the mystery. The location appeared to be the rebel's headquarters as the afternoon wore on, more black hummers parked in front of the valet turn. Several vehicles came filled with soldiers carrying automatic weapons, best they could tell.

The last car to arrive brought several unidentifiable people with bags over their heads. To Zack, it appeared the hostages were being paraded in front for their benefit. A large dreadlocked man in a glittering yellow Hawaiian shirt and bright red border shorts also emerged. Zack noted another male, possibly in a vantage point a tuxedo, greeted the other with an embrace.

Rod had sent photos back for evaluation.

"Why don't we do some recon?" Ken suggested. "Standing around waiting isn't helping the people held in there." Zack nodded. "If we could pull some out…"

Zack waited for Ken to continue, yet he stood silent. He stretched his arms, changing the seated position to a squat. From there, he raised his butt to the sky in a forward bend. A tapping rhythm broke the silence as Zack raised his body to a standing position.

"Where's Rod?"

"He left with the last bus," Zack swore under his breath. "Do we really need him?" Zack took the satellite phone out of his pocket. Ken watched as Zack typed in a short text. "I didn't know texting was allowed on this mission." Zack shrugged and waited.

In the silence of dusk, the phone's vibration brought both to attention. Zack read the text without expression. He glared up at Ken and then back to the text.

"Are you going to share?"

"Two words; what photos?"

"Son of a –

"My thoughts exactly." His phone buzzed again. His eyes widened. "Are they kidding me?" Zack mumbled. He looked back towards the tower. The phone is still resting in his palm.

"Do I want to ask?"

"No photos were sent," he repeated, "the sniper unit is being redirected to here, and it's now our job—

"To move the rest out?" Zack nodded. "Just me, and you?"

The phone buzzed again. This time Zack read the screen aloud, "14, 54, 9."

"Holy shit!"

"I am responding zero. Are you ready?" Ken nodded. His body still for the first time in what seemed to be hours. "Thoughts?"

Ken hesitated, "We are only seeing two sides. We should head passed the mall," he pointed as he spoke, "then look at the situation from the left and the backside."

"You've been thinking about this?"

"What do you think I do when I pace? Look, we are observing a heavily guarded entrance. My theory is they are lighter on the backside because who is going to attack from the water? They have an old destroyer anchored out there."

Zack's lips rose into a grin. He started to type. "We are, with back up." Pete's note was short. *I got an email from the sister. They are/were holed up at a joint near the landing spot. A team is on their way. Another coming in your direction. I may have a connection. Finish the job.*

"I like where this is going." The screen changed over to a map of the area as Ken came closer. Both men huddled around the phone as Zack explained a plan.

Celia's sobs penetrated through the bathroom door to float across the room and hit Ev and Rich out on the balcony.
"She's been at it for over an hour this time," Ev took a long drag off her cigarette.
"I've noticed. Can't you talk to her?" Ev frowned up at her husband. "You know what I mean, woman to woman."
"No, I don't." She brought her attention to the other tower. "I haven't seen the other man in days." Rich followed her gaze. "I wonder—
"Don't," Rich turned back towards the sobs. "We have other problems."
The bathroom door squeaked open. Celia walked back into the room. Ev and Rich watched her sit on the edge of the couch. She stood, walked towards the door, turned, paced back towards the sofa. Her butt hit the cushion with a swoosh.
"Hey, Ev," BANG! The door hit the opposite wall sending the three jumpings to a stance.

Maximum Trouble

"Come with me," a boy about sixteen pointed with the barrel of an AK-47. Behind him stood two others.

"Where?" Rich asked.

"Doesn't matter," the person in charge replied. "You are coming with us walking or in a bag." His companions laughed. Ev walked towards the kitchen as a flurry of Spanish sounded behind her. "I said, WALK!"

"I am getting my purse," she said as she reached for a small bag big enough for a pack of cigarettes and a few other items.

"You won't need," she looked up in time for him to catch her mom glare. "Fine. Get it, and let's go."

The three entered into the formal ballroom, now empty of most items except groups of people clustered around chairs set along the perimeter. A gathering of armed teenagers stood in a circle in the middle, talking to each other in Papiamento.

Rich, Ev, and Celia positioned themselves in one of the far corners. They took in the activities of the room in silence.

"I hate the waiting," Celia said.

"Me, too," Ev watched as her husband walk over to the other groups. With each encounter, a short conversation took place that ended with a shrug from Rich.

"What is your husband doing?"

"Making friends, as usual." Ev's focus volleyed between her husband and the teenagers. As Rich moved between the various clusters, the faction in the middle took note of every handshake and shrug. None moved to halt the interaction. Rich made his way entirely around the room. He sat in the corner with his back to the wall. "Making friends again?" Ev repeated.

"No," Rich answered with a growl. He lowered his voice. "Everyone here is from different hotels. No one knows each other. The kid from the balcony is over there," he pointed towards two women and a man seated across the room. "Other than him, I recognize no one."

"How did they get here?"

"Same as us, picked up by some militant people." One of the teenagers walked to a group of three women. He pointed towards the door. Hysterical cries echoed in the room as the three went out of view into the hallway. Pop, Pop, Pop. Then silence.

Maximum Trouble

"WHAT DO YOU MEAN THEY ARE NOT HERE?" Maxi woke to shouting outside the tent. Through a break in the canvas, she could see Harmony waving her hands in the air screaming at someone out of view.

"You show up here and bring your bad vibrations! Don't you care about your son and me?"

"I will ask you again, Harmony. And I want an answer," A bit of nausea rose in Maxi's throat. She tried to inhale through her nose to calm herself down. She turned to an empty tent. Swearing under her breath, Maxi frantically searched for another way out. "Where are the other Americans? I can feel they are here."

"Talin, you feel nothing! Look at you! What you have become! Have you thought about your family at all? What about your son? Your island? Can't you see what you have done to us!" The sound of flesh hitting flesh ripped through the air. "You bastard!" Harmony cried.

"Mom!" Maxi heard a scuffle. A scream. She backed against the far tent canvas.

"Ah, my son. Do not worry. This is our way with women. They are to serve, not question. My son, you should come with me to learn—"

"We agreed he would stay here with me." Harmony's voice echoed.

"Well, you should have thought about it... Moony, who is your friend?" Maxi crept towards an opening in the tent flaps. An oversized man in a Hawaiian shirt and bright red border shorts stood with his back towards her. His long dreads tied back with a purple ribbon, like Harmony's. His right arm rested on Moony's shoulder as his left-hand point to someone out of view.

Maxi's hand went to her stomach.

"This... Dad, you remember George. George, from the other side of the island. His mama—" Moony's words were cut off as the Rasta pushed his son aside. With two quick steps, a familiar squeal brought Maxi's hands to fists.

"And you are, George, you said Moony?" Maxi watched Ric nod, his eyes wide, through the break in the canvas. "And you are from the other side of the island?" Again, a wide-eyed nod. The Rasta jerked on his arm. "Liar!" he screamed.

"He is a lost boy. We don't know where his family is. He was wandering through the grass when Moony—"

"Silence!" The Rasta put Ric down, walked in a circle around him. He clapped his hands. "I must bring him to the Seaview."

"No, dad!" Rasta backhanded Moony with a quick flick. Harmony ran to her son's side.

"Yes. He will go to the Seaview. Yes. Today is go—" Maxi flew out of the tent and dived into the big man. Although out-weighed momentum carried her into his chest. He tumbled over onto the ground. Maxi turned to grab Ric as a giant hand gripped her shoulder to force her down to the ground. She scrambled as the barrel of a long rifle brushed against her nose.

"I knew there were others," the Rastaman smiled. "I knew that man couldn't be alone."

"Talin, please listen to me," Harmony begged. "this is all wrong. Let them stay with us. I will make sure they don't leave. Please, Talin."

He moved to Harmony's side. As if he didn't hear a word, he said, "Oh, my love, this island is almost ours." Harmony tried to move away, yet he pinned her body to his. "Tonight, we celebrate!"

"I am sorry," Harmony said, emotion leaving her voice. She watched Maxi hold her crying son as she and Moony stood by, helpless. Two men walked through the tall grass, one grabbing Maxi around her waist, the other helping Ric up and pointing towards the path.

"Take me but leave him," Maxi begged. "He can stay with Harmony. He is a good boy..."

"No mom—"

"Not now! Harmony, please!" Harmony looked away from the pleading mother. Her name is now lingering in the air.

The Rasta turned without a word. Harmony watched his bright yellow Hawaiian shirt disappear in between the long, green stems.

She didn't notice until now Moony had tucked himself under her protected arm. His body was flinching as quiet tears wet his face.
"Moony, love," she whispered as she rubbed his back.
"Why is daddy such a jerk?" he sobbed.
"Ah, Moony. Your dad was a respectable man until greed invaded his body…"
"You say that, but he's… he's… he's going to…"
"We don't know what he is going to do," Harmony lied. "We need to pray for our friends to be safe." Moony's head moved up and down against Harmony's stomach. He couldn't see the sadness running down her face. Nor could he see the blackness that invaded her eyes.

The long grass cut into Maxi's arms as the huge man pushed her through. She walked fast enough to keep Ric in her sight, yet the person behind her went more quickly. She could hear Ric's sniffles along with the Rasta assuring, "he would be fine."
The clearing overlooked the turquoise ocean. In another situation, one might say it was breathtaking. Soft white waves lapped into crisp, clean sand. A few palm trees scattered along with the Divi-divi's that make Aruba famous. A heavy hand pushed Maxi over towards a piece of driftwood. She sat with her

back to the field, twisting back at the tall weeds. She found Ric, sitting alone by the water. Rising to go to her son, the hand pushed her back down.

"You wait here," she's instructed. The Rasta sat in the sand next to her son. From her vantage, a civil conversation took place. She couldn't read their lips yet after a few minutes, both shook hands. The Rasta sauntered in her direction.

"Your son speaks perfect French," he commented as he sat next to her. He spread his legs, so his knees touched hers.

"We," Maxi replied.

"But you do not," he stated. Water hitting sand filled the silence. "I know who you are." Maxi didn't move. "And I know why you are still on the island."

"Then, please tell me." The slap came quick. Maxi started to topple over backward yet was caught by two enormous hands.

"Let's not be rude." The Rasta gazed at his hand. "Your friend, he was rude." He watched Maxi reposition her body facing him. "Yes, yes. We have your friend. Before you ask, you can go see him after we talk. I am not sure the boy should go, but that is up to you."

"The boy stays with me," she watched his hand rise, adding, "please."

"That could be accommodated. The boy stays with you, his mother?" Maxi nodded. "Yes, children should be with their mothers. That is why Moony stays with Harmony, at least for now." He turns to touch knees. "Where is the boy's father?"

"Dead." The Rasta leaned closer. "He was murdered by his mistress last year."

"For real?" Maxi caught his accent slip.

"Can't make this shit up."

"Huh." The Rasta surveyed back to the sea. "You are on our island illegally as Americans were told to leave. You, your son, and your friend will be brought to a detention center on hotel row unless you can tell me why you are still here."

"Mister, I'm sorry, what is your name?" He shook his finger no. "Well, sir, I would love to take my son and my friend and leave your island and never come back. This hasn't been much of a vacation for any of us. But I can't fix it. The airport is closed—"

"How do you know the airport is closed?"

"Because we were staying, in a cabana, on the beach, and when some guy showed up to tell us to leave, I asked for a ride to the airport, and he said the airport was closed."

"Some guy, huh?" The Rasta motioned for Ric to come. Maxi watched her son shuffle through the sand to sit on her other side. He slid his hands into hers. "You sure you want to bring him to see your friend?" Maxi nodded

as Ric's grip tightened. "So be it." He said something in Papiamento very fast. The heavy hand gripped Maxi's shoulder. "Follow my friend. We will move you later."
"Can we eat something or drink some water?"
"Ric!"
"Yes, he will bring you water and fruit." He nodded to the man standing by, then watched as they disappeared around the bend. He pulled a small phone out of his pocket. "I think I found the wife and kid."
"Are you sure?" he cringed at being questioned yet obediently answered.
"Bring them here. We moved them all from the rooms. The island is not, um how you say, stable."
"What about the electronics?"
"Fool! Do not speak of such over the phone! I will see you at dusk."
Silence.
Rasta smiled. He didn't have the codes. There was still hope.

L.M. Pampuro

Spencer sat in the far corner of the Omni Hotel bar. The vantage gave him a viewing range of Long Island Sound to his right, the New Haven green to his left, and anyone who entered the room in the front. He positioned his body to appear to onlookers as a relaxed one who appreciated the view. As others came, only his eyes shifted towards the movement. Wearing glasses helped keep this illusion.
He sipped an unsweetened ice tea through a plastic straw. *To hell with the environmentalists,* he'd toast whenever a waitress brought him the device. Most gave a hard smile back. He concluded they either didn't understand or didn't agree with his opinions. Either way, their tip came first.
As usual, his contact ran late. He glanced at his Rolex. *The next one he bought would be the more expensive choice,* he mused. The room grew noisier as time passed. He became intrigued by a younger couple near the

windows. Based on the position of their bodies, along with the eye contact, he concluded a break up to be on the horizon.

The woman would be more attractive if she smiled. The man kept folding and unfolding his hands on the table. He cheated, Spencer surmised based on his expertise. He missed the well-dressed woman scoot in next to him as water flew into the man's face. Soft laughter caught his attention.

"Next time use soda darling," the woman advised as the other stomped out of the bar. She turned to give Spencer a peck on the cheek. "Having a flashback, darling?"

"Not since I have been with you, dearest." To the rest of the bar, they appeared as an older, well to do couple meeting for an after-work drink. She slinked her arm around his shoulder to lean her body next to his.

"I'll have a vodka martini, straight up, with extra olives," she told the waitress before being asked. "And later maybe I'll have you," she lowered her voice. Spencer flinched. "Or not."

"Why are we here, Marjorie, and what's with the wig?"

"You didn't recognize me." He waited. "Plus, we never know who is watching." She flashed a new diamond tennis bracelet. "Our latest payment. A quarter-million is on my wrist." Her laugh carried as the waitress brought back her drink. She held up one finger while she took a sip. "This is acceptable. Now please bring me a side of olives because three," she pointed to the toothpick, "are not extra."

"Sure thing," the waitress vanished.

"Did you ever think about ordering olives with a splash of martini?"

The woman shrugged. "Spencer, darling, we have problems. Apparently, our friends haven't found their code... cocaine," she blurted out at the same time the waitress placed a rocks glass filled with olives down.

"Cocaine?" Spencer mouthed with a laughed. "She caught me by surprise. No matter. Our friends are still seeking the codes," she lowered her voice, "and based on today's meeting, have up'd their price."

"To what?"

"More than we can spend in a lifetime."

"Marjorie, we are in deep now. I mean before I could have covered us as an investigation, but now," he held his hand's palm up.

"No worries. I told them Brady was probably on the island. That got us this," she flashed the bracelet again, "and a little more time. We have a meeting with our contact here—"

"When?"

"They said they would be in touch." Spencer disappeared more into the shadow of the corner. Marjorie leaned further in, "Spencer, this is a perfect situation for us. Don't you understand? They capture Brady. He tells them nothing. We are fancy-free."

"Or dead."

Marjorie blew out a long sigh. "Can't you ever be positive?" She moved his chin, their eyes met. "Look, Spenc, this wasn't your idea. But think about this. If Brady didn't get assigned to the office, we would have been stylin'…"

"What does Brady have to do with all this?"

"Think about it, before he got here, we sent the occasional fleet local info, so their drug shipments could avoid the Navy—"

"And now?"

"Brady gave us access to a whole new dimension. Think about it. We could never have…"

"Can I bring you anything else?" The waitress's smiling face leaned a few feet away.

"We are set for now," Spencer said. "Bring the check when you have time.

"We have a free Happy Hour buffet set up," she turned towards the area where chaffing dishes sat, plates piled on each end. "Our drink specials—"

Spencer stopped her mid-sentence. "Just the check, please," he repeated. He waited until she disappeared into the now crowded bar area. "Brady brought access at a cost to our operation. Maybe I should have let him go on loan…"

"It wasn't him leaving that worried me—"

"Oh? Miss, I am going to destroy this desk until I find something useful?" Both laughed.

"Spencer, no! I mean, if he left, we might have been okay. Pulling his credentials—"

"So, this is my fault? I'm not the one who decided we needed to—"

"And I am not the one with the coke problem." Both turned their attention towards Long Island Sound. The waitress placed the folio upright on the table.

"Have a wonderful evening," she said as she vanished again into the bar area.

"Touché."

"Doesn't matter," she patted his thigh as he placed a fifty-dollar bill in the folio. "What matters is I came up with a way out." She sat up, triumphant.

"Do share," Spencer rose to assist Marjorie to stand. He caught the waitress's arm as she passed. "This is all set," he winked. He guided Marjorie out to the elevators. She started to speak. He cut her off, locking his lips to hers. "Not here," he mumbled.

"Gotcha," she mumbled back.

Maximum Trouble

Zack watched Ken Boci move around the buildings with precision. His gaze went from the cement structure to the inlets within his proximity, back to an overall arc of the area. Empty swimming pools with scattered lounges over-looking deserted beaches.

This is what they had hope for. "Something's off," Ken said. His voice a whisper. Zack gave a quick head nod. He followed Ken back into what should be a lobby area. "This is the structure next to the Seaview. Last I saw, there were snipers on the roof along with a few walking around in armor."

"There is no one here."

"Precisely." The two leaned up against the pink wall. Guns rested by their sides. "Where are our guys heading?"

"Here, they gave us two hours to move people out safely." Zack peeked out at the building closest to the Seaview. "We need to move."

Ken grabbed his arm to pull back into the shadows. "They are heading here? That's news." When Zack didn't react, he continued, "We need to think for a minute. I know you have this gut thing, well, so do I. I think we should go through the other building instead of the beachside." He pointed towards the opposite entrance. Zack nodded.

They walked in the shadows surrounding the pool area to dunk back into a cold cement hall. Sunlight danced in the distance as they moved through. About ten feet from the exit, Ken stopped to point. On the other side of the scruffy brush separated hotels, two men, both wearing semi-automatic rifles, leaned against the building. Smoke curled up from their lips. They spoke Spanish, at least from what Zack could decipher.

"Kids," he whispered. "They are talking about girls." Ken nodded. Neither moved. Another man, this one in an old Rolling Stones tour shirt, approached. He lit something, then passed it on. He said a couple quick words, pointed towards the structure they were under, and laughed.

Zack's eyes grew wide. "What?"

"He reminded the kids to move to the other side once the Americans arrive here."

"Why give up their position?"

Zack walked back down the hall, which they had come. In the middle, another hallway ran ocean to the parking lot. Zack pointed towards the sea, he moved in the direction, while Ken headed towards the front of the structure. A swish sound along with water hitting the sand, both filling the quiet yet not drowning out birds and other native sounds.

"Holy mother of God." Ken's voice carried. Zack sloshed back, stopping only to see the lighted end at the intersection of hallways.

"We're supposed to be—" Ken's finger pointed down to wires connecting boxes of explosives. "Holy…"

"Yep." Ken looked around for a transmitter. "There's the main wire. I would cut it—"

"But, we don't know if it is boobytrapped."

"I would bet the other side is hot too."

"Crap!" Zack pulled out a small phone, took a photograph. He typed frantically. "No wonder they let people this close."

"We need to move out of here," Ken instructed.

"We should wait—" Zack followed Ken's gaze. In the corner above the pile, a red light flashed. "Shit." Both moved with their backs against the wall towards the intersection. The flashing light stayed in one position as they went, with the rough cement wall at their backs, they slid around the corner into an inlet. "How did I miss that?" Zack's heart pounded.

"I did too." Both men glanced back at their route. They stood in silence, waiting. Ken smiled back in the direction of the camera as he pressed send on his phone.

Maximum Trouble

Pete walked back from the commissary, a turkey sandwich in one hand, a bottle of tea in the other. A vibration from his phone brought his lunch to the floor. "Oh, crap!" He bent over to pick up the wrapped package as he read the text. "Double crap!"

He practically sprinted back to command central. "We got trouble, boys." He connected his phone to the big screen.

"What the hell is that?" Commander Atwood exclaimed.

"According to Brady, we have a pile of explosives sitting in the adjacent building, wired, along with movement-sensitive cameras."

"Are they?"

"Yes, sir. From what we did gather from the insignias, made in Belarus. Favorites of pirates and drug lords alike." Pete stood to look at the screen closer. The pile of explosives appeared large enough to rip apart half the island.

"Pete, did Zack give any indication this could be neutralized?"

"Not that he knows of. Neither he or Boci were familiar with the set-up, sir." Atwood leaned back in his chair, hands folded in a triangle in front. He turned to pull up something on his computer, went back to the same position, now glancing between the explosives and his screen. "Sir?"

Atwood held up one finger. "Send this off to the SEAL team on the ground. The photo and location of the explosives. Can Brady still get in the Seaview?"

"They are looking for a place, sir."

"Stop with the sirs, already," Atwood said. Pete could see his commander getting agitated. "Tell Brady team two will handle the explosives. He is to stick with the plan."

"Got it, sir, sorry."

"And Malone,"

"Yes, sir."

"Word of advice; never hire a relative."

"You've met my family, sir. I wouldn't dare."A teenager approached as Ev lit a cigarette.

"Now you are going to tell me I can't smoke?" she glared.

"Over there," he pointed to another corner with smoke rising above. Ev took a long drag. She let the smoke float out in the kid's direction. She stood tall, walked across the room, with the lit cigarette swaying in her hand.

"I don't understand the difference," she mumbled as she sat in the only empty chair.

"Ashtray," balcony man pointed out.

"At this point, does it really matter?" He gave her a shrug back. The two smoked in silence with a half dozen others. Ev took a long, last inhale of smoke. She dragged the remainder across the ashtray. She stood to leave.

"Where are you all from?" The balcony man asked.

"Connecticut, you?"

"D.C. area," his voice low. "Walter," he extended his hand.

"Ev," she replied with a quick handshake. "My husband, Rich, walked around earlier." He nodded. "You on vacation alone?"

"My wife and son are," he gave a slow shrug of his shoulders to hunch forward.

"Yes, my daughter and grandson are, too." They both surveyed the room while keeping watch of the teenagers in the middle. Walter noted the group had shrunk since he arrived.

"Thank you for pointing out the cameras."

"No problem. It's what I do." Ev nodded back as if she understood.

"Well, I am going back by my husband. I am sure he will be by soon." She turned to leave only to walk into one of the teenagers making a circle. "Excuse me," she jumped back. He brought his gun up to eye level, positioned to shoot. "I am so sorry," she babbled. "Seriously, I didn't mean to..." A grin broke out on the boy's face. He laughed and kept walking.

"Asshole," Ev muttered as she moved back towards the other corner.

Maximum Trouble

The man in the tuxedo sat outside the ballroom surrounded by phones; arranged across the long table, all within reach: three cells, two landlines, one speaker. He waited. The only sound, an occasional laugh or shout, emerged from the closed doors of the ballroom. His guards mulled about, ready for his instructions.

He shifted his focus from phone to phone. The urge to yell "ring" each time, slid back to his skittish stomach. He dared to not look at a clock, making his situation into a game. *I will get a point for each minute passed. After ten minutes, I win!* He told himself. He started to contemplate prizes.

What shall they be? The safe passage from here. That was tops on the list. He couldn't wait to leave this horrible place. Of course, he will leave alone. That was a given. The helicopter would come to fly him, where? Where could he now go?

At least they did not know his name. Nor would they. His laugh caught the attention of his security. All moved to stand upright, guns were drawn. He waved them off.

This is power. The cellphone to his right buzzed at the same moment as a landline. He picked up the cell, said something in Spanish. He repeated the same phrase in Russian into the handset of the landline. Both disconnected at the same moment another cellphone range.

"Buenos dias, amor," he said.

"Buenos dias, love." Marjorie's voice crackled through. "Do we have our meet up yet?"

"Mi amor," his voice dropped, "Solo los poco mas largo."

"Bueno. I look forward to being in your arms again." They disconnected. Again, both the landline and center cellphone rang in unison. He picked up and dropped the handset back on the cradle at the same time flipping open the cell.

"I am almost done here," he started without any preamble. "When can we have a pick-up?"

"The Americans are getting closer. The airport is in shambles. We have our boat off the coast, yet by necessity, it may need to be spared like the others." He waited with silence. "My brother, I will be in touch early tomorrow with your escape route. Will you have the last piece?"

Maximum Trouble

"I will try."

"Try hard." He hesitated before checking to see if he was still connected. His brother wouldn't leave him here with the rest. At least he hoped not.

Maxi and Ric stood outside a tattered tent around the corner from where they started on the beach. The pungent smell of piss and something Maxi couldn't identify emulated from within. As Ric's grip tightened, she wondered if he should stay outside.

She pushed back the heavy flap. A whoosh of hot air encompassed both as the stench grew. "Wait here," Maxi instructed, disengaging her hand from Ric's. He stood still in the doorway as Maxi made her way inside. The sun shone through the frail roof, revealing an old wood table along with a couple chairs. Blankets lay scattered on the sand floor.

Huddled in the far corner lay two figures. As she got closer, the smell grew stronger. Maxi placed one hand over her nose as she reached out in their direction. Neither moved at her touch.

"Mom?"

Maximum Trouble

"Shush," she cut him off. "Please stay outside." Maxi moved further in. She pushed the blanket off the first person. A woman, maybe about her age, face bloodied. Her blank eyes stared up into Maxi's. "Are you…"

"I think she's gone," the voice low and crackled. "Sometime last night." Maxi brought her attention to the other figure, now sitting. Blood covered his face, and both hands were wrapped in gauze, tied together. He made noises while moving to sit. "Who are you?"

"My name is Maxi. I am here with—"

"Please don't say, Ric."

"How do you—" Maxi bent over to take a closer look. Underneath the blood and bruises lay Sam. She leaned in to give him a hug.

"Please don't," he responded as she recoiled.

"What happened?"

"Mom is that—" somehow Ric had moved to her side. Her hand again locked in his.

"Yes, it's me," Sam's graveled voice replied. "What the hell?"

"I could ask you the same."

"I got caught, taken here. They asked a lot of questions. I guess I flunked the test." His laughter turned into an explosion of coughs with spit spewing from his mouth. He raised his arm sluggishly to wipe his face.

"Is there water here?" Maxi scanned the room.

"No," Sam choked out. "No water. This one was here when I got here, barely alive. I didn't think she would make it through the night."
"Do we know—"
"I'm not sure." Sam groaned as he raised his body higher against the tent pole. "How did you both?"
"A kid led us out of the field. Turned out to be your host's son. Long story." Maxi dropped her voice lower, "We have to get you out of here."
"Ha! Good luck with that." Sam struggled to reposition his slumping body. Maxi noticed bruises going up and down his arms, disappearing under a ripped shirt. "We are on a beach, God knows where, with no transportation." Maxi opened her mouth to respond as Sam cut her off. "In business, we are in a hostage situation with little information."
"There is always—"
"Are you always this annoying?" Maxi sucked in a deep breath. Sam started to slide back down the tent pole.
"Yes," Ric answered. Both jumped. "She is."
Maxi moved back towards the tent flap. She rolled it up on one side, tied it with the hanging pieces of canvas. She did the same on the other. A faint, warm sea breeze made its way in. She looked back at Sam, slumped in the far corner, and sighed. The opposite

canvas appeared attached on both ends. Maxi untied the lower connection, rolled the flap up, and stood to hold it, with no way to tie the fabric back.

The warm breeze grew more robust, bringing in the heavy smell of salt and sea while pushing out death and despair. She glanced up and down the beach. In the distance, three jeeps sat parked in a circle, no humans present. In the opposite direction, nothing but sand, water, and Divi-divi trees.

"There is no one here," she said.

"They are here," Sam replied. He held up his hands. "This is why these are tied."

Maxi nodded as if she understood. "So, what do we do?"

"You and Ric may make it out of here, but not me."

"We aren't leaving Sam again," Ric stated.

Both jumped again.

"Stop doing that!"

"Doing what?"

"Sneaking upon us!"

"Mom, how could I sneak up on you when you are holding my hand?" Maxi looked down to see her hand still attached to her son's. "And we are not leaving Sam."

"We need water," Maxi ripped a piece of Sam's shirt off. "Let's cleaned you up a bit. That would help."

"Like putting lipstick on a gecko," Sam replied.

"When I was sick, my mom made me take a shower and dress because she said it would make me feel better. She was right," Maxi held back a tear, "so we are listening to Ev." She turned to Ric, "And if you ever tell your Grandmother I quoted her—"

"I know... I know..." Maxi walked towards the ocean. When she dipped Sam's shirt in, a pool of red emerged. She held back last night's dinner making its way back up her throat. She rinsed the rag. Maxi walked back to the tent to continue to wash Sam's face. He flinched with each touch.
"That stings!"
"But," Maxi kept moving the shirt around. "I need to rinse." She disappeared out of the tent.
"Is she always—"
"Yes," Ric answered. "I found it best not to argue at times like this." Sam laughed, then coughed.
"You are okay, kid," he managed to say. "You are okay."

Maximum Trouble

Marjorie and Spencer sat in the back of *Estas Merto*, a trendy Spanish fusion restaurant located deep in a not so safe section of New Haven. Marjorie took long sips of their homemade sangria. A half-empty pitcher positioned in front of her leaned against a mound of orange peels and cherry stems.

Spencer's unopened bottle of grocery store brand water weighed down his jacket pocket. The untouched filled glass the waiter had brought, sweated a puddle on the red, vinyl tablecloth. Their position gave a sweeping view of the entire room, out the full window, onto the street in front. Their car, with government-issued plates, drew a few passerby's curiosity.

"The natives," Marjorie swished her glass in the general direction. Spencer remained silent as they watched two teenagers wearing gray hoodies over their heads, walk around the vehicle. One slipped from view. Spencer counted to five, pressed a button on the key remote.

YEEP! YEEP! YEEP! Filled the air. The mid-afternoon lunch crowd didn't break from their conversations. If they had, observers would have seen three teenagers take off towards the heart of the neighborhood.

Spencer put his keys back in his pocket. "So much for being discreet," Marjorie slurred. Spencer slid the pitcher out of her arm's length. Mount fruit peel toppled, no one touch it. The waiter approached.

"May I take your order?" he smiled wide.

"We are waiting for friends," Spencer gave the same smile back. On the waiter, the look natural, on Spencer, forced. "Could you come back when they arrive?"

"Would you like something to drink while you wait?" The waiter persisted.

"We haven't finished our sangria yet. Maybe later." When the waiter turned his back, Spencer took the bottle of water out of his pocket. He took a long slip before he put the bottle back out of sight.

"Why do you do that?" Marjorie reached for the chips.

"Do what?"

"Bring your own water? Are rude to waitstaffs? Just an annoying pain in the...? I could keep going."

"Look, Margie," she cringed, "we are here to meet an associate who picked this location.

Maximum Trouble

Our business dictates we are careful," he glanced at her empty glass, "and have our wits about us. I take no chances."

Marjorie nodded, yet didn't reply. Her attention turned towards the door where patrons gave a full path to a small man surrounded by two linebackers. The big guys made their way to the bar. One sat facing the window, the other met Marjorie's eyes. She flinched. He smiled.

The small man pulled the chair out opposite Spencer, yelled something in rapid Spanish to the waitstaff, sat to turn his attention to the table.

"Buenos dias," he stated. His voice direct and quiet.

"Buenos Aires," Spencer returned. His lips curved up into a grin.

The small man laughed. "My associate told me you are funny." The waiter arrived back with a plate of steaming hot food. Behind him, another delivered a small cup of brown liquid. Three plates were distributed. "What do I have the pleasure?"

"You called us."

"Ah, yes. I did." He shrugged. "There is much happening. I believe you have something for me, no?"

"About that," Spencer leaned forward on his elbows. "We are having difficulties—" A small hand went up. At the same moment, the sizeable man facing the group stood.

"No hay necesidad," he quipped. The man sat back down.

"Good training," Spencer noted.

"The best," he replied. "So, you have difficulties. There are no difficulties. My people," he stopped to take a bite of the cheese/sauce mixture. "Bueno!" he yelled with a wave. The waitstaff let out a collective breath. "Your difficulties are, how do I say, not relevant. My people are in place. We need the information from you to finish. You have been paid to provide this information, no?"

"Yes, but—"

"There are no buts in my world. Your friend here," he nodded towards Marjorie, "said you would have what we need. Gifts have been given. Deposits have been made. Plans put in place," he took another bite, "there are no buts." Spencer moved to position the small revolver in his jacket. "And Mr. Spencer," the short man stood, "I would put your gun back in hiding. You see, my associates are everywhere. You won't make it out of your chair."

"Neither would you—"

"So, you say."

He walked out of the restaurant. The man facing the window followed close behind. The

other approached the table. He handed Spencer a card, turned, and left.
The front featured a photo of a downtown hot spot, the back, tomorrow's date, and a time.
"Finish tearing the desk apart again. Go through the middle drawer. If it blows up, so be it." Spencer said. He threw a fifty on the table, walked out with Marjorie practically running to keep up.

L.M. Pampuro

Both Pete and Commander Atwood jumped out of their chairs as Admiral Edels rushed through the office door.

"Skip the salute, men," he instructed. At the same time, his arm swept across the leather couch against the wall, sending take out containers flying. He sat down in the middle. "You boys are slobs," he noted.

"Yes, sir," Atwood responded, his hand stopped short of saluting. "We've been focused on the case." He started to pick up empty paper coffee cups, placing each with the others around the overflowing trash can.

"Good to know. Good to know." He focused on Atwood, "I hear you have news. I wanted to be here in person."

"Yes, we do." Atwood sat back down. "You are not going to like it—"

"Whether I like it or not is irrelevant—"

"Okay." Commander Atwood glanced in Pete's direction before starting. "Malone here noticed that one of the prisoners had a Russian Navy tattoo on his arm—"

"It took a while, but the boys on the West coast caught that one too—"

"Good to know. Good to know, sir. We made contact with an old colleague from those parts—"

"Old colleague?" Admiral Edels raised an eyebrow.

"Yes, someone we used on the Pacific rim job," the admiral shook his head. "He heavily denied any connection. Too adamantly if you ask me, so we went back into that file and found a loose link to a drug cartel in Turkey—"

"Is that all you got?" Admiral Edels rose to leave.

"Not quite," Commander Atwood gestured to Pete.

"Yes, sir," Pete jumped into the conversation. "We went back into Zack Brady's computer—"

"You went back into an F.B.I. secure area?" Edels raised another eyebrow.

"Yes, sir. I had a, we had a hunch somehow this all connected." Pete moved his computer to give the Admiral full view. "This is Brady's sign-in log to our site. He started checking in once the ship appeared off Aruba. You'll notice a second login to the same site, yet not from Brady's government or home computer."

"Interesting. Whose computer did the second logon come from?"

"Actually, sir, we are not completely sure." Pete glanced over at Atwood, who nodded back for him to continue. "It's registered in the New Haven office Brady had left."

"In the office. So, we don't have an actual person."

Atwood interrupted. "Not yet. However, we should have a location within the building soon. This will narrow down users along with logon credentials. We are almost there."

"Good to know. It gets my goat to think we have a traitor amongst our ranks." Edels rose. "I can't tell you how important it is to fix this mess A.S.A.P."

"We realize that—"

"Look, I understand we have family involved here," Edels attention directed at Pete, "but we need to lock this down. I'm going to give you the heads up your counterparts may have a name and a motive." Both men glanced at each other then back at the admiral.

"We have a theory here too. Are you going to share this information?" Atwood asked outright.

The admiral hesitated. "I am reluctant because of the family involvement," he stated, as he held his hands up to two gaped men. "You've seen the island updates… the explosives... the numbers able to be rescued... the numbers caught?" All nodded. "What is left out is we've narrowed this down to a militant group who in the past was paid money by smaller governments to avoid threats."

"Admiral, with all due respect," Pete began, ignoring the glare from Atwood, "this happens all the time. Why would a small group send ships and aggravate the United States?"

"Excellent question, commander." Edels sat back down. As he did, the other two followed. "All excellent questions." He folded his hands on his lap. He brought his attention to each man. "We live in a crazy world," he began, "surrounded by greed." Pete opened his mouth to speak, yet the scowl from his C.O. stopped his words. "These people have no scruples, obviously. On the last ship we captured, best we can figure, the captain shot and killed every member of his crew, execution-style. He posted photos on social media with the caption "The United States in action" underneath before killing himself."

"Is this similar to the forty virgins thing?"

"Not in any way. This son is not about religion. As I said prior, this is about greed. And these are awful, no horrible, people we are dealing with." He wiped his hand across his face. "If there is an internal connection, we must find it yesterday. In the meantime, let's bring our people off the island and help the citizens of Aruba take back their space." This time he rose, saluted both men before walking out.

Pete broke the silence. "Don, we need to finish this." Don looked back at the computer. "Get Brady on the line."

Maximum Trouble

Zack followed Ken out a back-service entrance into one of the thatch roof cabanas on the beach. Now visible to the ocean, the temporary hut gave shelter from the hotel properties behind. Ken peered around the side. He vanished into the next hut over. Zack followed a few moments later.

The two repeated the process until they found themselves at the edge of the Seaview. Signs indicated the beach of the private resort started about ten feet away. Instead of naturally made beach huts, the Seaview property had open, oversized, canvas umbrellas scattered about in different positions. In the middle, a small almost shed size wood structure, served as a bar.

Ken pointed towards the bar area, pausing behind divi-divi and palm trees as he moved. Zack made similar moves in a different pattern across the beach. Both met behind the shed. Zack watched as Ken took a long swing off a bottle of tequila. He offered it over to Zack, who shook him off.

Zack slid back to prop himself up against a palm tree. He pulled out a small set of binoculars and began to scan the hotel in front of him. He counted fourteen stories. Starting at the top, meticulously, he went back and forth, counting the number of rooms per floor. He repeated the process three times before crawling back to where Ken sat.

On his phone, he typed the information along with the locations of the three shooters he could see. He handed the phone back to Ken, who nodded as he read. "We need to split up," Ken's voice so low Zack could hardly hear him. "One of us goes after the guards on this side, the other," he pointed at the lone guard. "After we find the hostages…"

Zack shook his head no.

Ken blew out a loud sigh. "We both should—"

"If we both go and are captured—"

"We have a better chance with both our skills—"

"This is dumb." Ken stood and walked out towards the hotel. He strolled into the side door, and at the same time, the ground began to rumble. Zack ran towards the main property to take cover in a connecting cement building resembling a garage. The ground underneath him dipped as pieces of the adjacent building flew by right outside the door. One substantial chunk of concrete bounced on top of the small structure they had been inside minutes prior.

Sand, dust, and concrete flew by, encroaching on the entrance. Zack covered his mouth with the collar of his t-shirt before he placed his head with his hands. He crouched in the far corner feeling the rock and roll of the building on three sides

"*Funshona!*" Shouted out in Papiamento along with "*Dios ta aki!*" Zack stayed low in place. His phone vibrated in his pocket.

The ground stilled as silence rolled up along the beach, leaving only the sound of the wind and surf. The room accumulated sand while outside, as the dust cleared, pieces of pink concrete scattered the beach. The sun fought to break into the gray haze, now encompassing the area.

Zack remained huddled in the corner, against a concrete wall. Hands overhead, collar over the face. He waited in the stillness of the aftermath, taking in one slow breath at a time.

No birds sang.

No human laughter or tears.

Nothingness.

He stretched his body to a standing position. His hand slid across as he pushed up against the structure. The wall stood firm. Zack turned towards the opening in the door. Dust

entered diagonally, stuck to the far wall,
spread across the floor and ceiling.

He ran his hand around the back of his head.
His palm filled with pink dust. Outside, the
beach turned a pink shade of gray. Pieces of
concrete scattered about where lounge chairs
once lived. Sides of trees decorated in pinkish
gray with wires hanging. The dusted fog
blocked the blue ocean view.

He listened at the door. Still, no human
voices.

Where are all the people?

Maximum Trouble

Maxi tended to Sam's wounds while Ric ran back and forth, cleaning rags in the ocean. She found herself silently praying this wouldn't scar her son for life, yet Ric's actions showed more of his skills as a boy scout, then a child who will need a psychiatrist.

"How are you feeling?" Maxi inquired as Sam started to come back to himself.

"You should have taken off while you could," he barked back. "you don't know—"

"I can see you are feeling better," she wiped off her hands on the still bloodied towel. "Now, as far as taking off, do you think those nice young men with the guns down there will lend me a jeep?" Maxi laughed as Sam sat, mouth agape.

"Your mother is right," he said.

"What do you mean?"

"You do have a warped sense of humor." Maxi's laughter grew so loud Ric appeared in the tent door, out of breath.

"What's wrong? What's going on?" he said as he entered. He watched his mom is full-blown laughter, Sam shrugged in his direction. "Warped!" he added with a shake of his head. "Plain old warped."

Sam started to laugh as the ground beneath them rumbled. A boom sounded in the distance. "What the—" Maxi pushed passed Ric to move in the direction the sound emulated from. A dust ball rose up into the sky. She turned to see the boys on the beach piling into the jeeps. The roar of the engines, along with sudden movements of the vehicles, kicked up sand in all directions.

Two vehicles headed into the field, the third drove in the direction of the tent. "Company's coming," she pointed. Sam struggled to move towards the door. Ric helped him on one side, while Maxi took the other.

The jeep came to a stop, spraying sand everywhere. They watched a man, no more than twenty, swing his legs out the door. He spoke rapidly into a cellphone while keeping an eye on the threesome. "Yes sir…" was followed by "No problemo sir…" which follows another round of "Yes sirs." He hung up the phone, his gun in their direction.

"We must go," he instructed in broken English.

"Where?" Maxi asked.

Maximum Trouble

He pointed the gun in the air and fired a shot. "Now! *Ir!*" Maxi and Ric each grabbed one of Sam's arms. They maneuvered him into the back seat. The kid with the gun went back to the tent, fired a single shot before he returned to the jeep. Maxi mumbled a prayer for the woman left behind. The kid pointed to Maxi. "*Usted conduse,*" he instructed. Maxi stared back blank. "*Usted conduse,*" he repeated, this time louder.

"I think he wants you to drive," Sam mumbled.

Maxi climbed into the driver's seat as the kid jumped into the passengers. He positioned himself, so he could watch both Maxi and his backseat passengers. Maxi followed the tip of the gun as to which path to take. She bounced along a dirt road until it turned into paved. Within a few minutes, they were on the primary way that circled around the island.

Sam and Ric sat quietly in the backseat. They bounced around with each hit of a pothole. On their right, the Marriott property stood, lower walls covered with graffiti, the big M sign on its side in the brush. The kid pushed the barrel of the gun into Maxi's side. "Para!" he yelled. "Para!"

Sam mumbled, "This is it," although his words so slurred, Maxi could not understand. "Why are we stopped?" Maxi asked. The kid stared off into the grass. She started up the jeep to rapid Spanish and a gunshot. Ric reached over his mother to turn off the ignition. He held his hands up and said something in French. The kid scratched his head.

"You American, no?"

Ric replied with a French accent, "We are French American." The kid shrugged. "From Canada," Ric added.

The kid opened his mouth to talk as a big, black car pulled up. Talin emerged from the front seat. "Load them in," he instructed as the kid grabbed Maxi's arm. He pulled each from the jeep to lead to the back door of the car. They slid across cold leather seats. Goosebumps popped as they sat, shivering in the air-conditioned vehicle.

Maxi watched Talin take a handful of bills out of his pocket. He handed some to the kid, his finger pointed back towards the field. The kid watched the direction before driving away. The Rasta turned to eye each person, mumbled something, shut the door.

The car moved further into hotel row.

Maximum Trouble

Inside the ballroom, people screamed. The guards ran out as the building began to shake. They left the bewildered bunch of hostages standing in one corner. A booming thunder rocked the chandeliers. One losing its grip on the ceiling, smashed to the floor, throwing glass shards in all directions.

Walls, much like the occupants, cracked yet did not crumble.

"What the heck was that?" Ev said aloud. Her hand instinctively reached for a cigarette.

"Not thunder," Rich answered. He walked over to one of the walls to press his body against it. Walter followed.

"That was an explosion," he said.

Rich responded with a simple "Yep." The two watched a crack descend from where the chandelier started, down the length of the far wall. "It wasn't in this building—"

"Close. We should—" They turned back towards the twenty or so remaining people in the room. Their captures had left through the far door. That left three exits to choose from. "If my orientation is correct, our friends went out towards the front of the building." He pointed towards the far wall, "that door should bring us to the casino—"

"And the one behind us to the beach." Rich smelled cigarette smoke. His wife had lit up amongst the others. "The beach maybe patrolled." He nodded in the direction of the smoke. "Also, depending on what blew up, the beach might be more challenging to move across."

Both men walked back towards the group. Rich reached over to a cigarette extended within his reach. He took a long drag, handed it back without a glance. "Casino or beach?" he asked as if the day is typical.

"You choose," the reply he expected.

"I say casino to the opposite exit," he said. "Or at least in that direction."

"Always the casino with you, isn't it?" Ev gave a toothless smile in her husband's direction. He took her free hand in his.

Walter gathered up the non-smokers. "We need to try while it is still quiet. Once they come back—" All nodded. "Rich," he nodded in the direction of the door.

"How the hell did we end up in charge?" Rich's voice just above a whisper. He and Walter lead the group towards an exit. "I learned not to volunteer in the Army."

Walter laughed. "Yeah, my dad gave me that advice too."

"You're retired military?"

"Something like that," Walter turned away before Rich could ask anything else. "Let's do this."

The door opened easily, leading into an emergency light lit hallway. The group moved as a quiet unit in the direction of the hotel's mass casino, yet whimpers and gasps echoed from behind. Rooms flanked both sides with names like *Turtle Cove, Sunset Landing,* and *The Sand Pit.* Underneath the last, an idealist photo of a child sitting with a pail and shovel on the beach. Both Ev and Celia paused at the image as they passed.

The smell of mold, something rotted, and body odor lingered with each step, stronger by some doors, weakened at others. The hall got brighter as they moved away from the ballroom. As rooms passed, walls became more pink and turquoise green. Lights flickered, indicating the end. To the left, darkness. To the right, grayish-blue dust hung in the air.

Walter nodded towards the dust while Rich pointed in the opposite direction. "This direction leads outside," Walter instructed. "We don't know where that goes," he pointed towards the darkness.

"The dust came from the explosion, I am guessing," Rich said. "I'm thinking we should head in the opposite direction of whatever caused it." Walter hesitated. Ev pushed by to move to her husband's side.

"Which way?" Rich pointed towards the unknown. She walked into the hallway until she disappeared. "Well?" echoed in the dark. Rich shrugged before he followed into the darkness. Celia and a couple others trailed behind. A shadow flickered in the light at the opposite end. Walter moved the rest of the group out of sight as a person's outline came into view.

Maximum Trouble

Ken Boci got inside the Seaview as a loud boom shook the foundation. He moved fast, staying in the shadow as he made his way into the main hotel lobby. Standing behind a substantial floral display, he watched a mass hysteria of people, mostly young men, run through the room, out the central doorway. Each a touch of the wild in their eyes along with a semi-automatic rifle in their hands.

Some yelled in **Papiamentu**, while others forced their way by. Last through came an entourage lead by the small man in a tuxedo. He spoke rapid Spanish as he smiled back at the four NFL sized linebackers who surrounded him. Each held a toothless grin that did not reach into their eyes. Boci observed that the tuxedo man spoke a softer, Slavic language when he addressed his bodyguards.

The group made a leisurely stroll across the lobby, stopping only to be met by a fifth member, a Rasta in a Hawaiian shirt, and red

Bermuda shorts similar to Ken's. He carried a black case. Boci noted the chain to his wrist.

He thought he was home free until the group stopped and took up residence in a circle of wicker chairs that faced out the floor to ceiling front window. Although he couldn't see the full view, what Boci could see appeared as a front-row seat to watch the world crumble. He delayed a few more minutes, waited to see if anyone else joined or left.

The conversation slowed, sounding more leisurely than pressurized. At the current pace, he could catch a few words here, and there he almost understood. Boci slipped back through the hallway, to head down the stairs back towards the beach. Behind him, screams faded. In front of him, whispers echoed.

He took a cellphone out of his pocket, typed a quick message. *Your brother holds court in the lobby.* His phone buzzed back. *The others?* He gave the location of the group moving through the lower level. *I'll take care of my brother. You do your job.*

Boci moved his head from side to side as he reread the text. He took one last glimpse at the man holding court before he disappeared from view. Not for the first time, he mumbled, "If only government work paid."

Maximum Trouble

The door flung open, banged against the frame, sending both Atwood and Pete jumping out of their chairs. Atwood's gun is drawn in his hand.

"What are you, an idiot?" he shouted at the M.P. He placed his firearm back in the top drawer of his desk.

"Sorry, sir," the young man stuttered as he saluted. "I was told to get down here at once." He hyperventilated a few times before he continued. "There was an explosion on the island—"

"Where?" Pete cut in.

"Building next to the Seaview. If you—"

"On it," Pete's hands soared across his keyboard as he punched in coordinates. Atwood moved to his side. Satellite photos showed a hole where the other hotel once stood. Pete zoomed in to see damage on the facing side of the Seaview, yet the building remained in tack.

"Were any of our—"

"No, sir." Now the M.P. stood at attention reciting his report. "Team One was in transit," he pointed to a moving dot on the screen. "They are cutting off the escape roads in case anyone from the Seaview attempts to leave." He points to across the island where another dot is moving towards the hotel. "Team Two had dropped off another group and was in the process of heading back."

Both men looked at each other. They waited for the messenger to continue. "Any other news?"

"Not at this time, sir. Intelligence thought you should have more than a phone call because of the situation." Both men nodded.

"Thank you for delivering the news in person." The M.P. saluted, turned, and left. Pete plugged in a few other coordinates. He waited for his screen to catch up.

"Are we still getting signals from your father's phone?'

"The signal is faint, yet there." He pointed to a different screen. "It looks like the phone at least is still within the Seaview."

"Pete, is the signal moving?" Pete zoomed in the area of the pale dot. As the position got clearer, both could see slow movements towards the water. "This is good, no?"

"At least we can see the phone is on the move." He reached over to his satellite cellphone. "We've got some news," he barked in the speaker.

"Me too," Zack Brady answered back. Zack sat out on the beach, leftovers of the hotel in full view. The remains of the Seaview, along with the rest of the beach, floated in a greyish-blue breeze.

"Glad to hear your voice, buddy," Pete added. "Is Boci with you?"

"No. We split up before the explosion. Was that—"

"No. You guys didn't set that off either?"

"Nope. We got on the Seaview property and were making our way across. Boci chose one route and me another. I was in a concrete bar when it happened. What about the rest of our team?"

"Both on the route from other areas."

"Good to hear." Zack listened for voices before he continued. "Boci is inside, I am walking the perimeter. I don't see anyone out here. Even the guards on the side of the building disappeared." Zack leaned over to brush dust out of his hair and off his hands.

"My dad's phone is still giving a signal from inside the building."

"Do you have a location?"

"I will send this to you. It looks like whoever is in possession of the phone is moving towards the beach. We also have both teams on the way, so if you can get them to a safe point, we

can arrange a pick-up."
"Good. Pete, do we have any other information about who is doing this and why?" Pete glanced back at Atwood, who nodded no.
"Not yet, brother. I will be back in touch." They disconnected. "Why—"
"Not yet. We have a connection to his old office, but they are not the masterminds. We can't chance it Brady will freak out—"
"I've known Zack for years. He is cool under pressure—"
"You also are aware of the protocol, Pete. We have to wait." Pete nodded. He brought his focus back to scanning photos and data.

Maximum Trouble

Rich felt Ev's hand in his as he made his way along the wall, each step secured with caution. Ev had Celia's hand on her shoulder, as the others did the same, building a chain stretched back to the corner where the venture began. The walls damp with air conditioning sweat, provided little assurance as they moved in the right direction.

A soft glow formed about forty feet ahead. Rich slowed the pace as he approached. The light emulated from panels on outsized commercial washers and dryers. Canvas bags of sheets and towels stacked up in one corner while moving shelves of the same items, folded, lined the other.

The group squeezed to fit inside.

Walter forced himself into the doorway. "Anyone got laundry to do?" he half-joked. He could see Rich narrow his eyes in the direction of where he stood. "There's another door over there," Walter pointed behind one of the shelving units.

Rich followed his finger. "Well, I'll be damned," he muttered, moving in the direction. He put his ear to metal and listened. "I hear engines, but they don't sound close," he said as he leaned on the handle. The door cracked open.
"I wouldn't do that," Ken Boci's voice startled the group. The big man's body filled the doorway they had entered.
"Who the hell are you?" Rich barked. He watched as the group from the ballroom crowded into the opposite corner from where the stranger stood. He noted Walter had moved to the back of the group, out of sight.
"I could ask you the same," the stranger replied. As the silence grew, Rich moved towards the front. Others continued to work at opening the door further. Ken did not move or offer additional information. He peered over his shoulder, back from the direction he had come, several times, yet brought his glare back decisively on Rich.
"I'm here to help you," Ken broke the silence.
"Then tell us who you are."
"I can't. I have to make sure—" The door wedged open, sending the metal frame banging against the cement. Walter moved fast, slipping out into the bright sunlight. He ran along with the building towards the beach, slipping on the sand, hitting various pieces of debris along the way.

Maximum Trouble

Walter sprinted around the corner of the structure, out of view from the others. He tried to catch his breath as his body slips into a squat against the building. He put his head into his hands.
"Who the hell are you?" brought tears. He thought he had escaped.

The smell of body odor and human gas enveloped the car within minutes of arriving at the Seaview. The Rasta and the driver disappeared inside, leaving Maxi, Ric, Sam, and another severely beaten person in the back. With no air conditioning in the blazing Caribbean sun, the seats condensate while the occupants turned to puddles.

Maxi punched the buttons to lower the windows. When that didn't work, she jammed her fingers between the rubber seal and the glass. Neither moved.

Her vision blurred. People's faces faded in and out. She turned to Ric, who slid in the seat next to her. The sweat from his body had soaked his clothes.

"Come on, baby," she encouraged, "stay awake for me." Ric would give a toothless grin as his eyes went to half-mast. "No, no, no, no, baby. Listen to mama. Let me see those baby blues." His smile widened as his eyes further closed.

Maximum Trouble

Maxi brought her feet up and started to kick at the window.

"Save your energy," muttered Sam, he too slumped off in a corner. "Save your energy..."

Maxi took inventory of the car. Four people, three fading, way too freakin' hot... She looked in every direction. A small mini bar was attached to the driver's seat. She tried to wedge her finger under the partition to put all her strength into the motion. Her fingers sliced against the glass, yet she managed to move it about a half-inch.

"Not good enough," she said.

She went back to the contents of the minibar. There were three canters. She took a sniff at first, a bottle of clear liquid, the distinct smell of rotting fruit. She picked up the bottle of golden liquid. It stuck to her hands. The last one, an empty bottle, smelled like vanilla. Four glasses, three of which had the sticky remains of something, were arranged in square holders. A mini-fridge contained a bucket of melted water along with an empty can of Coke.

All useless.

As Maxi slipped back next to Ric, her foot hit bottom. Something substantial fell to the floor. Sam perked up. "What was that?"

"I am not sure," she answered. Maxi reached down to place her hand around a foot-long metal rod. "Jackpot." She reached back to slam it against one of the windows at the same time Sam stopped her forward motion.

"What is the plan?"

"Smash the window, get air in here, escape, be rescued, live happily ever after," Maxi replied.

"Seriously. We need a plan and as wonderful as yours is..."

Maxi brought the rod down. "Sam, we are suffocating in this car. We need fresh air."

Sam nodded. "Could use this to try to pull down the front panel further, but we'll still be stuck in the car."

"Can you see inside the driver's area?" Maxi nodded. "Look to see if there is anything useful for us in there. If so, go for the panel."

"If not?"

"Still go for the panel. Unless there is a guard on us, we can get an idea of where we are and what our next step should be. I would hope the driver's area won't be blacked out, like here."

Maxi followed instructions. Using the rod as leverage, she managed to lean on to the panel, adding another four inches to her view. "I'll be damned," she leaned further on the rod, obtaining three more. "They left the keys in the ignition."

"What else do you see?" Sam wiggled himself closer.

Maximum Trouble

"We are in the valet drop off of one of the larger hotels, I'd guess on the row. I don't see people, although I am sure they are around."

"You are sure?"

"Gut. Don't ask." Maxi tried to lean in further. "I need more weight here."
"I'll help, mama," Ric stumbled to the front. He knocked into Maxi, the rod flew from her hand.
"Dammit!"
"Mom, I am so—" Maxi held her hand up.
"My fault," she said. Turning towards Sam, "I think we can do this with fingers. A few more inches and I can crawl through." Sam raised one eyebrow. "The plan is to open this up enough for me to get through. I will start this mother up, hit the gas, and we will get the duck out of here!"
"As long as you have a plan," Sam replied. He positioned himself on the opposite side as Maxi. His fingers ached as he gave what was left of his energy to pull down on the divider. Maxi grunted next to him. The divider gave way to send both tumbling against the wall.

Zack repeated the question in perfect Spanish, *"quién eres tú"* to which Walter swore under his breath. "Come on, buddy, I am here to help." From experience on both sides of the current situation, Zack could see a debate going on inside the man's head. "I really am trying…"

Walter brought his attention to this new person. "My name is," he hesitated, "Rich. Rich Malone."

Zack's lips turned up into a grin. If this person knew Rich, he might know their whereabouts. "Rich Malone, you say," Zack answered while reaching to shake hands. "Is that so?"

Walter hesitated yet shook hands. "I didn't catch your name?" he replied.

"Ah, my name," Zack broke into a full smile, "I am Joe," a code used on his last mission to identify others in the same position.

"Joe, you say," Walter answered. "Glad to meet you." Both men stood with arms folded, volleying their gaze between the ocean and each other. "Where are you from, Joe?" Walter never was good at a quiet contest.

Zack kept the smile as he answered, "D.C., you, ah Rich?"

"Ah, the same." Walter shifted his weight from side to side, he scanned back in the direction he had arrived from. "I think we should get out of here," he added, sounding more like a question than a statement.

"Huh. Yeah. I agree." Zack let out a laugh, "Funny story, I know a guy, maybe twenty years older than you, same name, much different attitude."

Walter froze. "Where's this guy from?"

Maximum Trouble

"You tell me. Of all the fake names you could have chosen…"

"Shit," Walter swore. "Are you really from D.C.?"

"Yes."

"Did my father-in-law send you?"

"Who's your father-in-law, Rich Malone Senior?"

Walter smirked. "No. Don Atwood."

"Admiral Donald Atwood? Shit." Zack pulled out his phone, took a photo, and hit send, the whole while shaking his head. "How do you know, Rich?"

"Rich?" his eyes popped open. "Oh, Rich Malone? Hey, wait, you really know Rich Malone?"

"Yes."

"Oh man, of all the names I could have pulled out of the air," Walter peeked around the corner. "Rich, Ev, you know his wife," Zack nodded, "and some other people, we were stuck in this tower," he pointed up at the Seaview. "When the explosion happened, we took off. Rich was in charge,"

"No doubt—"

"We got to the laundry room on the side down there as someone—"

"Who?"

"Some guy in a Hawaiian shirt. Showed up. I snuck out the back—"

"Why?"

"Because I don't know him and going back to being held at gunpoint didn't appeal to me."
"Understood." Zack's phone buzzed. "Brady," he listened to the voice on the other end, his lips bent up into a grin as he handed the phone to the other guy. "It's for you."
"Walter," he said his name as he reached for the phone. "Hi, dad." Zack turned away. "I left it with Gigi." As the conversation continued, Zack slipped around the corner. He could make out people in the distance yet not faces. He counted twelve outlines with more coming from the side of the building, the last a generously proportioned presence with a drawn gun.
"We got to move," he turned back to Walter. "Now." Walter handed the phone to Zack. Admiral Atwood's voice came in clear, "Good job, Brady, now I need—"
"Sir, I don't mean to interrupt, yet we have a situation here. It appears your guy Boci has about fourteen people lined up behind his drawn gun."
"Are you sure?"
"Positive. I need to move," Walter mouthed his name, "Walter, to a safer spot. I will go back—"
"Brady, we have people on the way. Continue on your mission—"
"But sir, I think that—"

Maximum Trouble

"Your mission, son." Zack squeezed his eyes shut. "And Zack, thank you." The phone disconnected.

Zack placed the phone back in his pocket, turned to Walter to ask, "Who is Gigi?"

Marjorie rushed passed Spencer's secretary, slamming open his office door. Spencer sat behind his desk, one hand covering his ear, the other stuck to his phone. He looked up at Marjorie, pointed to the door then back at the chair by the side.
He indicated for her to lean in as he positioned the phone, so both may hear. "Do you understand the implications?"
"Yes, sir," Spencer responded. He rolled his eyes in Marjorie's direction.
"I expect you to take proper action." Again, he gave the same response. "And Spencer, they are keeping a close eye on your entire operation. Do not embarrass the organization."
The phone went dead before Spencer could respond.
"Who was that?" Marjorie asked as she moved to create distance.
"D.C."

Maximum Trouble

"Who in D.C.?" Spencer rolled his eyes. "Shit." Marjorie blew out a breath. "This can't be good." Spencer started to speak yet stopped. He reached into his desk to remove a small pistol, aiming it in Marjorie's direction. "Spence, you are joking," she said as she waved her hand to push it away.

"I told you from the start I would not take the fall for this."

"And I told you we wouldn't get caught. Just calm down and put that thing away." Spencer put the gun on the desk, resting his hand alongside. "I have to think," Marjorie stood to stretch her arms over her head. This action caused her skirt to ride up above her thighs. Spencer took in a glimpse of her lace panties. "That is what got you in trouble in the first place," Marjorie followed his eyes. She brought her hands down to fold in front. "What do they know?"

"They are aware someone besides Brady tapped into the Pentagon site and went into classified information."

"Okay," Marjorie pursed her lips. "That is a start. But they don't know who or what computer?"

"It's a matter of time." Spencer leaned back in his chair. "We may need to update our exit strategy."

"We may, or we can go in one more time, try to get what we need, and then…"

"One more time, you say?" Spencer rubbed his forehead before adding, "Why not. Did you get in touch with the hacker?"

Marjorie stopped moving. "Hacker? I thought... oh." Her lips curved into a toothless smile. "You are a genius."

Maximum Trouble

Zach pointed to the garage he had hidden in early. "Go there and wait for my signal," he instructed. Walter stood still. "Go there—"

"I want to help," he said.

"And you will be staying out of my way. Just go there, please." Walter moved in the direction Zack had pointed. Zack watched for a minute before bringing his focus back to the group on the side. He could hear Boci yelling instructions.

"I am looking for the Atwood party of one," he shouted. "Atwood? Atwood?" Boci broke into a weird laugh as his hostages stared at one another.

"I think you got the wrong group," someone from the back answered. Boci brought his weapon in the direction of the voice.

"I don't think so," he sputtered. "Who said that?" His face turned bright red. "I SAID..." He went back to laughing. "That's okay. You'll be my first, later."

Zack repositioned his body in between a sizeable piece of concrete and a divi-divi tree, in the sightline with Boci along with most of his group. Zack counted thirteen total. He glanced back to see Walter peaking around the corner from his hiding place.

Zack pointed back towards the inside.

"Okay, who is next in the lottery, Jacobs? Do I have a Jacobs?" Ev let out a yelp. Boci stepped in her direction. Rich pushed his wife back. "Why'd she make that noise?" He brought the gun up in Rich's face. "WHY?" he shouted.

"I have no idea," Rich answered.

"I do," Boci grinned. "She's a Jacob." He reached around to grab Ev's arm at the same time Rich pushed him back. The crowd parted at the sound of a gun firing.

"Son of a—" Fire rushed through Rich's foot as he fell to the ground. Ev dived down with him. Boci pulled her back up.

"Not you, Ms. Jacobs," he laughed. Celia squatted next to Rich. She helped him sit against the building. "Is he really your husband?" Ev's eyes grew as the gun skimmed her chin. She nodded. Boci's smile grew. "The rest of you can go," he said. "I don't need any of you."

The group stood still. "GO!" he screamed. He watched the bodies scatter. "Let's move him.

He may still be useful." Celia and Ev both took an arm over their shoulders. They lifted Rich the best they could.

"He needs medical attention," Celia stated.

"Not where you are going," Boci replied. He pointed back towards the hotel.

Zack crept along the tree line. The gunshot brought Walter back out. He had followed at a distance. He tried to melt into the trees as people ran passed. He watched the disoriented move down the beach.

"What do we do now?" Walter's voice broke his concentration.

"You are going to stay here and waited for the tactical team one to give an update. The photo I took of you has been distributed so you will be recognized."

"And what about you?"

Zack pointed towards the laundry room entrance. "I am going to get my in-laws." He turned back towards Walter. "Any others I should be looking for?"

Walter choked, "My wife and kid are out there. I left them at a hotel in the middle of the island. A couple green berets were there with their family too. I hope…"

"Next stop," Zack said as he moved back towards the building. The trail of blood stopped inside the laundry room. The sound of wheels scraping on concrete grew faint in the distance. Zack turned the locator on his phone from the current channel to one he and Pete use.

He moved along the cement walls in the shadows, as the smell of mold lingered. Down the far hallway, the squeaking wheels stop. The distinct sound of an elevator door opening resonates. Once the sound passed, Zack moves towards a stairwell off to the side. The clambering of wet sneakers against metal stairs resounds to the first exit. He stops at the door to listen.

Silence.

Zack repeats the process to the second floor. Here to he is reached with more silence. The stable door offers no visuals. His soft touch moves the handle until it gives a soft click. With a tender push, the door opens about an inch.

Faint voices linger. Zack opened the door enough to slide his body into an empty hallway. He followed the sounds to a balcony overlooking the lobby area. From this vantage, he observes several men sitting in a circle in front of a large window. Just behind them, he counts four dressed in black, all armed with automatic weapons.

Zack moved towards the grand staircase, crawling along the far wall. Close by, an elevator door opened, followed by the sound of wheels moving. From his position, he could see a laundry cart with a slumped body inside, being pushed by Ev and Celia.

The portly physique of Ken Boci came into view behind, gun drawn.

Ken said something Zack couldn't quite understand at the same time two men took their attention away from the window. One had on the same clothes as Boci, a bright Hawaiian shirt with red Bermuda shorts. The other dressed in a tuxedo. A third man now joined the group. He stood off to the right of the rest. Zack noted his eyes in motion, circling the room.

"What is this?" Boci's twin inquired.

"Talin, don't you recognize the Jacob family?" Boci answered.

"I thought the Jacob girl was in the car out front?" the man in the tuxedo injected.

"She is," Talin answered. "Who are these people?"

Boci let out a hard sigh. "The one pushing," he pointed his gun at Ev, "Yelped when I asked for Jacobs." Ev gave a blank stare back. "The one in the hamper jumped to her rescue and the other one," he looked at Celia as if seeing her for the first time. "Who are you?"

"I'm their daughter," she answered to silence.

"Doesn't matter. And in your car?" The man in the tuxedo asked.

"I have a girl, her son, another lady, and a man," Talin's voice grew quieter with each admission.

"Bring them here," Tuxedo man commanded. "Then we go," he said back to the man scanning the room, who nodded in reply. The group moved more into view. Zack took and sent a photo then moved closer to the stairs.

Maximum Trouble

The window let go sending Maxi headfirst into the driver's seat. Ric scooted over after.

"Mom," he said, "mom, mom, mom—"

"What?" Maxi yelled. She swung her feet around, missing his face by inches.

"People are coming out of the hotel," he said. Sam launched half over the partition. In the passenger's side mirror, three men emerged, guns drawn, followed by their capture.

"Max, if you could get it started and hit the gas…" Maxi twisted the key. The engine came to life. The three leading the charge stopped to position their guns in the direction of the vehicle. Their capture charged forward.

Maxi jammed the gearshift into reverse, backing the car over two of the gun holders. The third lost his balance, falling against the building. Their capture screamed. Maxi moved the car into drive, shrieking wheels propelling the vehicle forward, into the other vehicles scattered within the valet area.

Rapid gunfire pinged off the back window,

causing cracks.

"Maxi, move!" Sam shouted. Maxi's hands slipped as she tried to hold the wheel tight. The car slid around the tight circular driveway only to move back towards the hotel's sliding doors. Ric's body volleyed between Maxi's side and a hard slam against the passenger's door. Sam noted others had emerged from the lobby. "We have a party," he said. "Some are shooting. Some are pointing. Oh, crap, Maxi! Watch out for the—"

The car hit the pole head-on. From the hood, smoke sulked out from the sides. Maxi's head smashed into the steering wheel. She heard Sam yell "Crap" before her world went black.

Maximum Trouble

Atwood and Pete followed the dots moving across the computer screen. When both merged into the same area, the two men high fived. "Finally, a decent connection," Atwood noted. Pete nodded yet didn't answer. He kept his focus on the screen.

"I just got word team one picked up about ten people about a mile or so down from the Seaview. They are on route cross island. We are waiting on a debriefing."

"Good," Pete responded. "Is anyone we know in the group?"

"We don't know at this point. Team two captured a group of young men who say they were guards at the Seaview."

"Aren't you suspicious of the information?"

"Pete, these are scared teenagers…" Pete, again, shook his head up and down. He typed in different coordinates to see movement across the island. The two dots representing Zach and his father remained close, in the same spot.

"They're not moving," he pointed to the screen. Atwood looked over his shoulder to where Pete pointed. "The dots are in the same position for about a half-hour now. Brady hasn't been in communication, awe crap!"

The photo appeared blurry, yet Pete could make out his mother, another woman, and Ken Boci in the foreground. "This is why they haven't moved." He could hear Atwood yelling at someone. The phone handle hit the cradle hard.

Pete watched his commanding officer throw papers off his desk while a tirade of audible swear words escape from his lips. Breathing heavy, he stopped mid-sentence. Methodically he picked up every sheet of paper. He placed each in an empty recycling container. He arranged his pens in order of length.

Atwood brought his concentration back to Pete. "Sometimes, I can't believe the idiocrasy I hear," his smile fading, "We have the New Haven connection."

"Why do I think I am not going to like this?"

"Because this is stupidity in action." Pete glanced back at the photo. "Ken Boci went to school with Marjorie Spicer."

"Which one?" Pete asked as his conversation at the house with Zack started to come back.

"Does it matter?" Atwood ran his fingers through the little hair he had left. "Brady's former secretary in New Haven, I can't believe no one," he threw his hands up, "seems the two were married—"

"Married? But that doesn't mean anything—"

"Pete, the breach in security came from her computer."

"Okay." Pete pointed to the photo. "I am guessing both are loyal to a different party than ours?"

"Ken is a missionary. He does this for the money, nothing more. I found out his discharge from armed services wasn't honorable."

Pete's fingers clicked on his keyboard. "Huh," he replied as he stared at the screen. "I can't find a recommendation on file. Who hired him?"

"Again, stupidity in action. The Team One leader—"

"Rod something?"

"Yeah, him. Recommended to the team—"

"But Zack called, and we had confirmation—"

"That we needed someone who knew the terrain, especially because of the volatility of the situation." He watched as Atwood's fingers pounded his keyboard. The commander silent as he went. "That Rod something gave a list of ex-patriots who would help out for cash he used prior." He went back to thrashing. "Both Rod and Ken have a connection to Bosnia—"

"Bosnia?"

"—via Russia." Pete watched the screen as the rhythmic hammering ceased.

"We are in a precarious position here," Atwood began to explain. "The last report said they had moved about three hundred people. None of which are 'our' people, unfortunately."

"Zack has Walter—"

"Zack left Walter in a safe place. Walter, who is not the sharpest tool—"

"Isn't Walter your—"

"Son in law. Baby girl met him when I was stationed in Guam. He was some sort of computer science geek then," he stopped to take a drink of his room-temperature tea. "Now he's a cybersecurity expert. Carries his personal computer with him everywhere." Atwood let the thought sink in.

"Personal computer, sir?"

"Yes, the personal computer he uses to hack into secure sites, for fun, he tells me." Pete sat back to focus entirely on what Atwood was saying. The son-in-law hacked into a secure site at The Pentagon then downloaded a bunch of codes, "one of which is the launch sequence for Nevada."

"Shit!"

"Precisely. And dipshit didn't realize what he had and kept them on his computer."

"If you don't mind me asking, what did he plan to do with those?"

Maximum Trouble

"I have no idea. Most of the communications I have been receiving is about the progress of the code change. Because of the hazardous nature of the circumstances, this is taking much longer than it should get fixed."

Pete tapped in a few keystrokes. The two dots appeared to be moving towards the water. "They're on the move, sir," he reported back.

The sound of crushing metal drew the front circle outside. Curiosity assisted in moving the armed guards behind. Zack waited all of ten seconds before he slid down the stairway. Without a word, he grabbed Ev to push her in the direction of the back door. He pointed at Celia to follow.

Rich was shaking and sweating inside the hamper. "Hold tight old man," Zack said as he pushed the hefty basket out of view. He directed all towards a long hallway into a back staircase. "Rich, can you walk?" The older man nodded no.

"Just leave me with a gun," Rich winced as he tried to sit up. "I will shoot whoever comes near and—"

"No," Zack cut him off before he could finish. "Hang tight. Ev and—"

"Celia,"

"Celia, go to the bottom of the stairs here. Check if anyone is at the bottom." Both women descended the metal staircase. With a firm grip, they pushed on the door, which squealed in response. The hallway appeared dark and empty.

"We're good," they reported back.

Zack moved the hamper to the top of the stairs. "Hang tight, Rich," he said. "I am going to do my best to not let you crash." Between the weight of the basket and the person inside, Zack concentrated on moving down the steps as meticulous as possible. His arms burned as his grip kept slipping with each downward step. The cloth started to rip, leaving a more pronounced trail of blood.

With two steps to go, his grip gave away. Rich launched forward, yet by some miracle, the hamper stayed upright. The wheels bent inward, uncooperative, yet able to move, Zach rammed it through the door.

"We need to get to a place where I can see his leg," Zack motioned in the direction of the water.

"That bastard shot him in the foot," Ev explained, barely able to catch her breath as she spoke. "We were in the ballroom, and there was an explosion," she panted as she tried to catch her breath, "Rich lead the whole group out. We were almost outside and then this asshole,"

"To say the least," Celia added.

"This asshole pulled a gun on us and started asking—"

"For Maxi's last name, right?"

"And I made noise," Ev started to cry. Zack maneuvered the hamper into a storage room. Packages of towels, canned goods, along with bags of rice and beans, lines one wall. Three aisles of metal shelves divided the area. Paper plates, tiny soaps, and cardboard boxes filled the space.

"Ev," Zack pushed Rich into the far corner out of view. "look for a first aid kit, aspirin, bottles of water, and bring me some of those clean towels. Celia, take a few of those ketchup bottles and squirt them in the opposite direction from the stairwell. You don't have to go far, make sure to leave a trail."

Both women went about their assigned duties, Zack brought his concentration to Rich. "Okay old man," he said, "don't leave me now." He cut the back of the hamper then eased Rich out onto the floor. "Can you move?" he asked. Rich's eyes had moved down to slivers. He leaned his head back, hitting the wall with a thump.

Zack brought chairs to each side, then moved his torso in an up position. He disappeared through the door, bending the hamper apart as he went. Inside the stairwell, he piled the remains into the corner, not visible from the top.

Off in the distance, he could hear voices, screaming in Papiamento. He found Celia almost to the other side of the building. He gestured her back. Zack closed and locked the door behind. Ev had Rich's foot raised up on a third chair. A pile of bloody towels lay near. She had several first aid kits along with a couple bottles of rum close by.

Rich groaned with each touch. Zack stood back to take a photo then hit send. He gave coordinates before moving the bloody towels to the trash. By now, he could see Ken's bullet had dismembered the baby toe. The wait caused a great deal of blood loss.

"See if there is a sewing kit in any of those boxes," he pointed at Celia. "Okay, Ev, what do we have here?"

"He's fading out Zack. We need to get him to a hospital, and even then—" Zack held his hand up to stop her midsentence. He repeated his request. "I worked with the elderly who rarely came in with bullet wounds," she started to say. "His baby toe is shot to pieces. The bleeding subsided some. Keeping his foot elevated will help. We need to—"

"Here's a sewing kit," Celia pushed into Zack's hands. Without explanation, he withdrew a needle and the cardboard thread holder. He reached for the rum, opened the bottle, to spill the fragrant liquid over both pieces. He then handed the bottle to Rich.

"I am aware you don't drink, yet you may want a sip or two while I am doing this." With no response, Zack turned to Ev, "Keep him awake. Slap him. Talk to him. Try to not yell as we don't want any attention."

"What about me?" Celia asked.

"Take all the gauze and bandages out. See if there is any rubbing alcohol anywhere." She nodded. Zack moved with the precision of a surgeon. With each insertion of the needle, Rich flinched, yet he did not pull away. Zack connected the flesh. He spilled a little rum over the wound. Rich yelped in response. Celia had accumulated a pile of gauze.

"Hold his foot up, I'll be right back." After washing his hands in the shop sink in the back corner, he wrapped up Rich's foot, When Ev moved aside, all could see the color starting to return to their patient's face.

"—And now onto plan B."

Maximum Trouble

Harmony and Moony arrived at The Paradise to find men in camouflage circling the property. They watched yet didn't approach the two as they made straightaway for Malaya's office. She sat in the back, in her private garden. Another young mother and child by her side.

Harmony greeted her in their native language. "Please speak English in front of our guests," Malaya instructed.

"Sorry," Harmony spoke as she walked over to an empty seat. Her Caribbean accent was more prominent as she got closer. "Harmony," she extended her hand towards Gigi, who squeezed it yet didn't reply. "Moony, why don't you take the boy to auntie's pool." Moony opened his mouth to object. "That wasn't a question."

Gigi nodded to her son. She watched the two boys disappear into the courtyard. While the others began to talk, she moved away.

"Why are you here?" Mayala crossed her arms as she sat back in her chair. Harmony made the opposite move to lean closer, her hands rested in front of her knees. She watched Gigi for a few minutes before answering.

"Talin is out of control," she started. "He not only took a mother but her child too. I can't—

"You can't what?" Gigi brought her attention to the conversation. Harmony sat agape.

"The woman asked you a question, Harmony," Mayala wasn't going to make this easy for her.

With a deep inhale, Harmony answered, "I can't let him continue. I need to... I need to..." She wept, her head down in her hands.

Mayala rolled her eyes, still creating distance with their bodies.

Gigi spoke, "Who is this mother and child?"

"The boy's name is Ric, I can't remember the mother's. All I know is Talin is inhabited by an evil force—"

"It's call greed," Mayala chimed in.

"And I have to stop him."

"Why?" Gigi had moved close enough to touch Harmony yet barely out of reach if she needed to be. "Why now?"

"He took the boy—"

"So, the others didn't matter?" Mayala now leaned a bit more in her direction. She watched Harmony twitch and turn, her eyes now as red as the palms rubbed away her tears. "Answer me! My Phillippe is gone! Others who were brought here, gone! I have your crazy husband harassing me in person and by phone, and let's not forget the soldiers—"

"What soldiers?"

"The soldiers who come by at night. They disappear into the swamp behind us."

"There were soldiers on the island?" The two jerked at Gigi's voice. "When did they get here? Are they Americans? Can they help us?" Both watched Mayala as they waited for answers. "We hear them at night, and the watchmen have seen them move through the tall grass. A few have stopped then moved on. The night soldiers do not scare us. The day soldiers," her eyes fixated on Harmony, "the day soldiers threaten my family. My friends," she gave a quick smile in Gigi's direction, "go into hiding. The day soldiers once were family…" She stopped. They could hear an engine coming closer.

Mayala gave a quick chin nod to Gigi, who scurried in the direction of the boys. "If you do not want to be seen with me, you should follow her," Harmony stood.

"Will she hide the boys?" Mayala nodded. "Then I must go contrary to my name." She disappeared in the direction of the parking lot, returning moments later with two semi-automatic rifles. She handed one to Mayala. "We need to stop this now."

L.M. Pampuro

Maximum Trouble

Ric's body slammed against the door. His elbow connected with the locks. Sam used his left hand to wedge the door open. "Ric, climb in back and follow me!"

"My mom!"

"Don't worry," as the words came out, Sam pulled the driver's door open with a haunting scream. He pulled Maxi from the car, over a cement wall, to fall down into a deep dam, out of sight.

Above the breaking glass, a bombardment rhythm reverberated only to bounce back from the mall structure across the street. Sam pushed Maxi's limp body further out of view. He brought his hand up at the same time Ric's grabbed it.

With wild eyes, Ric asked, "What are you doing? She saved you!"

"I am trying to save her. She needs to—"

Silence cut off Sam's speech. He brought his fingers to his lips, then pointed upward. In a whisper, "Your mom is still breathing. We

need to bring her to, but not here." He motioned towards a concrete tunnel. "Do not make any sounds." With a grunt, Sam swept Maxi's body over his good shoulder. He limped towards the dark circle, Ric's loud breathing indicated he followed. The murky water deepened as the light disappeared behind.
"Sam, where are we going?" Ric's voice quiet. Flesh hitting flesh followed. "Damn bugs," almost by habit adding, "Don't tell my mother I said damn."
Sam laughed, and although Ric couldn't see, he smiled, his face muscles ached from the gesture. "There are a lot of damn bugs, Ric." Ric's hand rested on Sam's shoulder. The water began to reside at the same time, walking became labored. The cement bottom sloped upward, yet the end not visible.
Maxi's limped body, along with Sam's awkward movements, started to take a toll. His left knee buckled under the pressure. Both landed on the rough surface with a thud. Ric tripped over the two bodies, falling alongside. He scrambled to reach out to touch Sam.
"Sam?" the question floated in the air.
"Crap," Sam answered. "Are you okay, kid?"
"I think so," Ric moved closer, "Maybe a scrap. You?"
"My knee..." he stopped talking.
"Mom?"

Maximum Trouble

"Right here. Let's try to get her to wake up," Sam put his finger under Maxi's nose. He experienced a weak yet warm airflow. He exhaled. "Ric, could you move around me. I am going to set your mom next to you." Ric sensed his way around Sam, who positioned Maxi next to her son. "I need you to hold her up." An outline of Ric confirmed movement to the affirmative.

"Hi, mom," he whispered. "Sorry I—"

"No apologies," Sam interrupted.

"Sor-, sorry, Sam." Ric put his free hand over his mouth.

"Just start again, kid…" Sam tapped Maxi's cheeks. He put his fingers along her wrist, her pulse, like her breath, weak yet present.

"Mom, I love you, and we are going to be okay because we always are okay and we have to be positive but mom," he stopped to gather his thoughts, "I think the next time we go away in the winter we should go skiing because then we can't get stuck and I know it is more work, but I promise to ski with you, and maybe I can teach you how to ski the trees…"

"Ski the trees? What's that?" Sam moved around to position his body in front of Maxi's. He placed his hand on her stomach and pushed. Her body jerked forward.

"Mom!" Ric yelled. Maxi lurched forward. Her mouth opens as gritty bile spewed out, covering all three. "Oh crap," Ric covered his mouth, "I'm going to be sick." The smell of body sewage filled the cavern. Maxi whimpered then fell silent.

"Don't breathe out of your nose," Sam instructed. He repositioned Maxi once again over his good shoulder. He took Ric's hand to place on his weak side. "We need to move." Sam coughed then spit off to the side. "Up or down," he mused. Ric pulled in the direction they already experienced.

"The devil, you know," he mumbled.

Maximum Trouble

The helicopter landed beyond the mall, over by the abandoned strip of stores where Team two had set up a mid-station. Most of the group moved on the route between the drop off at the far side of the island and the Seaview. Rod stood alone in the field, making hand motions. He, the sole provider of where to land.

He saluted the one occupant who disembarked. Then in perfect Russian, "**Privetstvennyy Komandir** Arcadio," when no answer came, he switched to Spanish, "Hermoso día en la isla, ¿no?" (Beautiful day on the island, no?) The commander gave Rod a sly smile. He waved in the direction of The Seaview.

"I am here to fetch my brother, so the day is," he let the thought linger. In perfect English, he continued, "Did you take care of our minor problems?"

Rod shifted from side to side as they walked towards the convenience store. Two dead bodies lay off to the side, both with half a head missing. "Sir, I have done my best. Your brother—"

"Ah, yes, my brother." The commander shook his head. "His impetuous caused me many sleepless nights," he stopped to meet Rod direct into his eyes, "but family is family," Rod responded with a quick nod. "So, your minor problem…"

"The hotel is secure. When I left to meet you here, the Malones were in the lobby. Boci had to shoot the patriarch, but he is alive and can speak."

"What about the others?"

"We had the hacker—"

"Had?"

"Yes, sir. Boci—"

"Get rid of him."

"Who, sir?" Now the commander moved faster in the direction of hotel row.

"Just get rid of him. This Boci person. His work is done." He waved his hand in the air as if Boci was dead. "Now the rest… I need the hacker. Without the hacker this," he spins in a circle, "is all a waste of my government's time and my money." Rod followed as the commander moved through the mall's courtyard. "I have people waiting. Do what you need—"

Maximum Trouble

The two came to a sudden stop across the street. Several men in black surrounded a car as their semi-automatic rifles filled it will bullet holes. Off to the side, his brother stood in a full tuxedo, next to two men who wore typical island attire. Several more men in black ran up, saluted, and were waved off as they ran in the opposite direction.

"Take me back to the helicopter," Commander Arcadio kicked the sand.

"Pardon me, sir?"

"Take me back to the helicopter. My brother turned this into a *cogida de grupo* as you Americans like to say." His pace quickened. "I am done here. Unless you can bring the hacker to me now," Rod walked into his back, "you are done here too."

"No comprende, sir." Rod reaches behind his back to finger the gun under his shirt.

"Kill your darlings," Commander Arcadio laughs. "Kill your darlings." He mounted back into the waiting helicopter. He hung out of the door to add, "You have twenty-four hours."

Rod watched the helicopter take off in the direction of the hotel. It circled once around the Seaview before releasing a rocket. The smoke trail was ending somewhere behind the building. The explosion quivered under his feet to vibrate back towards the U.S. landing spot.

He listened to the shouts coming through the mall. He heard another explosion ricochet over the water. Rod stood planted in the one spot, unable to move.

The ceiling crumbled above as Zack attended to Rich. He watched as toilet paper, shampoo, and cans of beans tumbled off the shelves.

"We need to get out of here," he said, at the same time, he helped Rich to stand. "Can you walk?" Rich shook his head. "Then I will carry--"

"Leave me." Rich slumped back into the chair. "No," Ev answered. "Now, get up off your ass and let's go." She made a move towards the door. With her back turned, Rich scrunched his nose and stuck out his tongue.

He pushed up off the chair, tears materialize in the corners of each eye. He grunted to a standing position. Zack brought one arm over his shoulder to guide both out the door. The pathway to the beach blocked by a jagged piece of concrete. Zack pointed into the familiar direction they just passed.

"This way." Ev arrived to take Rich's other arm. She mumbled something about putting him on a diet if they survived this mess. Celia carried a pillowcase filled with ointment, gauze, and water bottles. Instead of taking the stairs, they continued straight. Shouting could be heard from above.

Maximum Trouble

A large metal door signaled the end of the passage. They propped Rich up to catch their breath. A bar, locked into place with a rusty padlock, blocked their entry. Zack leaned Rich up against the corner. He pulled a knife out of his socks and started to chip away at the metal.

"Do you really think this will work?" He turned to see Ev, cigarette in hand, positioned over his shoulder.

"Do you have a better idea?" She shrugged in response. Celia stayed focused on the direction they had passed. The knife slid. Zack swore under his breath. His face red, he turned and back kicked the door, breaking the seal. "I'll be damned," he said as he moved the bar to push the exit open.

The dark, cement tunnel had about a foot of water visible. Movement on the opposite wall caught his attention. He moved the door to shine what light there was in the direction. "Are you kidding me?" he said as he jumped into the water.

Pete watched the unmarked helicopter launch a rocket into the beachside of the Seaview. Minutes prior, team one confirmed they had picked up Walter. They were on their way back to the meeting point. The dust blocked most of the view, yet when the U.S.S. Dolphin One shot a rocket in retaliation, the boom of explosives hitting the target lifted his spirits.

Don Atwood disappeared about ten minutes prior, mumbling something about a meeting. He said he'd be back as soon as possible. Pete had sent a message to Zack about Team One. No reply.

The screen with both Zack's and his dad's phone indicated where ever they are, they are together. He still waited on word from his sister.

His screen beeped. Another update from Team One; *Priority One has been brought to the landing. We are heading back for the others.*

Maximum Trouble

Team Two is out of contact. Pete read the last part twice.

Atwood returned to the news. "Something is up there," he said after reading the exchange for himself. "The F.B.I. took Marjorie Spicer into custody. She is singing like a bird."

"What about Spencer?"

"He is currently M.I.A."

"And guilty?"

"It seems so. If these two and Boci were the internal connection, then we should have what we need—"

"But—"

"Something doesn't fit. That explosion you saw. Intelligence tells us Benedito Arcadio was on board. Him and the pilot."

"Isn't Arcadio the drug guy?"

"Drugs, and much more. We now have word he was working with Belarus and Lebanon on something."

"Something, sir?" Pete chuckled. "You said two of the top five countries who have major issues with the United States. What was he trying to do, be an arms dealer?" Atwood raised his eyebrows yet didn't respond. "Seriously? He was trying to move—"

"Degads, I think he's got it."

"Walter." Atwood nodded.

"When that dumbass boasted on the hacker's forum he is always on, Arcadio did his research. We've tracked payments back to familiar operatives, including some in the New Haven area."

Pete peeked back at his screen. "Our friends?"

"Friends of friends."

"Where do my parents fit into all this? I mean, they're just retirees."

"Yeah, that," Pete's eyes opened wide.

Commander Atwood's voice filled the room. "Wrong place. Wrong time." Pete started to giggle. "What's so funny?"

"They'll blame my sister."

Maximum Trouble

The soldier entered the courtyard with a pistol resting in his right hand. Mayala and Harmony stopped their conversation mid-sentence.

"If you come any closer, I will shoot you," Mayala's voice much calmer than her stomach.

"I mean you no harm," the soldier raised his hands in the air, still holding the gun. "I am look—"

"For crying out loud," a voice boomed behind him. "That's Mayala. She owns this place and helped me and," a full eek turned attention to the flash that ran by, "Gigi!" he yelled at the same moment he caught his wife's body in his. "Gigi," he sighed into her hair.

Her muffled tears appeared contagious as both Harmony and Mayala wiped their eyes. "How did you? Where are? Oh my god!" Gigi became incapable of finishing a sentence. Another scream brought Cole around the corner. They lifted him into the center of their cocoon.

Mayala turned to the soldier who saluted her. "Team Two of the United States recovery unit," he identified himself. Others made their way into the area, guns rested by each side. "Are there any others here?"

Harmony and Mayala exchanged a glance. "There were, but they have gone." The soldier nodded. "Are you searching for anyone in particular?" He shook his head no.

"Mayala, you remember Walter," Gigi dragged her husband over, "and this is Harmony." Walter acknowledged both with a soft bow. "Mayala helped Cole and me." She tightened her fist to bring hard against her husband's arm. There was enough force to cause him to massage the spot after. "And you are an idiot! Did you know my dad—"

"What about your dad?"

"I haven't talked to him yet, but I bet he's going to be mad!" The soldier faced the other direction to snicker. "See, even he knows," Gigi called him out.

"Harmony and I have work to do," Mayala shifted in her chair. Harmony said nothing. She watched the exchange. Most of the soldiers had left the area, yet the one remaining lingered within hearing distance. "Don't you have someplace to go?"

Maximum Trouble

"Mam, we do. I must ask if you both need refuge too. We are willing to take you to safety but," he glanced down at her skirt, "you need to leave your firearms here." Mayala again moved, this time she brought the rifle into full view.

"We have work to do," Harmony answered for both. "We need to take out, how you say, garbage."

"We can help you remove," he smiled, "your garbage if you'd like."

"It is our garbage. We must do this," she answered.

The soldier nodded, thanked both women, then disappeared from view. Once around the corner, he instructed, "See if you can find out what they are up to," to one of his men, "stay out of view, yet..."

"Got it, sir," he saluted.

L.M. Pampuro

Tuxedo man watched the helicopter land behind the mall. He waited with expectancy for his brother to see what he had accomplished. The man with the codes was close. He could work around it. He had hostages the U.S. would pay for along with the island itself. That would earn him respect.
He glanced in the direction of his operatives. Both would need to die. His only decision would be together or separate. The native screwed up getting the girl to him, although it might not have been the one he sought. He shook his head. A burst of maniacal laughter escaped from his lips. *Who leaves keys in the ignition?*
No bother, he gestures in the direction of the bullet holed car, no one could have survived. Another laugh escaped. Over his left shoulder, the native watched him through half-closed eyes. Over his right, the American's pupil's darted in all directions. Maybe he will let his

brother decide who will be the first. He could
even give him the honor—
Wait, what is that...
From behind the mall, the helicopter rose
again. He peered in between the buildings
across the street, yet his brother didn't
appear. Through the dust, he can't see who
sat inside, yet the outlines of two figures
brought his fingers to his temples.
The loud sound shook the hotel. It knocked
loose the cement footings. Chunks of cement
fell from above. The vibration stopped his
guards from shooting. Another rumble
followed by a tornado of dust engulfed the
area.
His guards ran, screaming, in all directions.
He stood still. His feet planted solidly on the
ground. He waited for the silence for after
mayhem; the silence always followed.

Sam couldn't see who moved towards him. The light from the door provided a temporary blinder. "Ric, stay close," he instructed. He stood tall and with an audible grunt, brought his hands up. He braced what little energy he still inside for a fight. Maxi's body lifted from his shoulder at the same time Sam brought his arm back to swing.

"Stop," Celia's voice cut through the rumble.

"Celia?"

"Who's ya think it was?" she waded through the water to help him hobble into the hallway.

"Celia," His face wet from sweat, the moisture in the corners of his eyes still visible. "Celia," he repeated. His good arm held tight to her shoulders as the other dangled by his side.

Ric ran towards his grandmother. He stopped short when his Papa came into view. Ev scooped the boy into her arms. "I am so happy to see you," she squeezed his small frame into hers.

Maximum Trouble

"Me, too," Ric tightened his grip. "Grandma, is papa?"

"No!" She turned Ric towards her husband propped up in the corner. "Rich, look who's here—"

"Your favorite—" Ric finished her sentence. Rich winced then forced his lips into a grin. The "hey" he returned their greeting barely audible. Zack placed Maxi's still limp body next to her dad's. "Mom," Ric lunged in her direction as Ev pulled him back.

"She's alive," Sam said. "Hit her head hard on the steering wheel when the car hit the cement pole. She has a pulse and is breathing—"

"She talks sometimes," Ric added.

"Yes, she has been speaking words." Sam caught Zack's eye and mouthed. *She needs a doctor.* Zack pointed at Rich. He raised his hands up then same time taking a human inventory. He took out his phone and typed, *The band is back together. Three maybe four need MD's a.s.a.p. See locator. Send...* He looked back down the hallway towards the front of the hotel.

"Where did you come from?" He directed at Sam. His task not yet complete.

"The other side of this starts down an embankment at the main entrance," Sam moved closer. "The opposite direction is a dead end. It might have had an exit before the last explosion."

Zack separated from the group to examine the tunnel in both directions. "I wouldn't go back in there," he added.

"Yeah, we puked in there," Ric said.

"No shit," Ev added. "I thought the smell was your mother's new perfume."

"Grandma," Ric stood hands on hips, "pick on mom all you want when she can answer back, but now is not the time." He brought his attention to his mother before he could see his grandmother start to cry.

"Wiseass. Like mother like son," she noted as she riffled through her purse. "I'm out of cigarettes."

"God help us all," Rich stated as he sunk lower in the corner. Zack sent a second message reading *Out of cigarettes. Hurry!*

Zack walked down the hallway towards the front staircase. He could hear his group reconnecting more than halfway down. He focused his listening in the opposite direction. Nothing but silence. Where the hallways merged, emptiness in both directions. He walked back to stand outside the group, like two lures, his eyes moved back to Maxi.

He could see her chest moving, yet her head rested against the wall with no participation in the on-going discussion. She didn't respond when he picked her up or when he whispered, "I am so happy to see you." She needs a doctor. Rich needs a doctor. The other guy over there needs a doctor, maybe Ric too.

"I hate to break up this reunion," he coughed out, "but we need to get out of here." Those who were able nodded. "I'm thinking between the three of us who are healthy, we can move the ones who need help." Again, head nods. "Since the tunnel is, what did you say, Ric?"

"Full of puke."

"Yeah, full of puke. I think we should go back the way we came. When we get to where the two hallways meet, give me a minute to go ahead to figure out what direction."

"Do you have a means of communication?" Sam had somehow moved to the opposite side of Zack.

"Yes. And I have sent two messages to explain our situation, especially the lack of smokes," a nervous laugh circled. "Right now, we have two teams on the island. One should be dispatched in our direction." A few nodded. "Ev and I will continue to assist Rich. Ric, are you able—"

"Don't burden the kid," Sam said. "Celia and I can help with Max..."

"Are you sure?" Sam brought his body to a full stance. He looked direct into Zack's questioning eyes. "Alright then," Zack

motioned. He took Rich's weak side to place his arm back around his shoulder. Ev lifted the opposite. Sam and Celia got into position.
"Hey, what is my job?" Ric stood with hands-on-hips.
"Carry this," Celia pushed the pillowcase with the medical supplies and waters in his direction. Ric grabbed the sack. He threw it over his back. He signaled with a head nod back to Zack.
"Let's go."

Maximum Trouble

Harmony drove down the pitted back roads with such ferocity Mayala found herself praying they made it to their destination in one piece. Two semi-automatic rifles, along with a case of bullets and a couple of pistols, rolled around in the back seat.

"Can bullets explode if they are dropped?" Mayala inquired at the same moment her behind bounced back into the seat. Harmony kept her eyes on the road. She mumbled something incoherent back. "Just curious because we keep hitting—" Her head banged against the rollover bar.

"No," Harmony said. "They cannot explode in the box. I am more worried about missing that bastard then being blown up." They both saw the helicopter and rocket across the flat island. They both had felt the ground shake, heard the rumble, and watch the dust rise into the sky.

Inquisitiveness, along with cold hearts, kept the forward motion towards the mayhem on the opposite side of the island. Harmony had snuck around the front of the office and lifted two additional guns out of the soldier's jeep. She let the air out of two of the tires before she heard voices approaching her direction.

Once Harmony mentioned Phillippe, Mayala wanted to go. She made Moony promise to stay out of sight until she returned. "An hour tops," she promised. When he asked where they were going, she answered, "off to see the wizard." He knew better than to request more.

Harmony slowed the jeep as The Seaview came into view. "I don't see anyone," Mayala said.

"Doesn't mean they are not there." She drove slowly around the bend then into the driveway of the hotel next door. She cut the engine. "We should walk from here." Mayala agreed.

Mayala placed the rifles to lean against the jeep. She took out two boxes of bullets, loading each gun to capacity. At the same time, Harmony loaded the smaller guns. "We should take extra," Mayala handed her a small box, which she placed in her pocket.

Both women strapped a rifle over their shoulder, then placed the smaller guns into the waistbands of their shorts. Mayala dropped a pistol into her purse. She wrapped the bag city-syle across her opposite shoulder before she stretched for something on the floor of the front seat.

The two women looked at each other. Mayala had a bright, flowered floppy hat covering her head, a pink gauze shirt, Bermuda shorts, sandals, a straw purse over one shoulder, and an AK-47 assault rifle over the other.

Harmony's long hair tied back in a loose bun. She wore a purple and blue spiral tie-dyed shirt with shorts like Mayala's. Blue Nike sneakers, her own AK-47 across her left shoulder with a small pouch across her right. She leaned into the jeep to remove the keys, throwing the set under the car.

"Just in case we both—"

"Not going to happen, sister," Mayala said. "Let's get rid of the cockroaches."

Around the corner, two soldiers from Team Two watched the women. One took photos "because no one is going to believe this story," while the other observed their actions.

"There is proof women drive crazy," the first soldier said. "I thought we were going to flip a couple times," the second man nodded, "For the record, I still think we should identify ourselves, go and help them..."

"I think they would shoot us if we approached," the first pointed out. "We can follow at a distance to make sure they don't get stuck in any crossfire." The women moved into the foliage. The two soldiers close behind.

One spoke quietly into his walkie-talkie, the other moved branches aside to pass.
Just beyond the garden wall, behind the bullet-ridden car, three men stood in conversation. They pointed at the vehicle, then beyond. One man turned in their direction. He held his head in his hands and shook his finger back at the other two.
The soldiers scanned the area. They were alone in the garden.

Maximum Trouble

As the operation became more intricate, all essential personal crammed into a conference room adjacent to Admiral Edels' office. Six people, four computers, one projector, and a coffeemaker share the space. Each screen focused on a different area. Pete had the movements of Zack Brady and his father in front of him. The next screen showed the aircraft carrier off the southern coast of the island. A third gave a satellite view of the hotel and the last communications with the two teams on the island.

The last screen projected onto the far wall. "Team Two, location accepted," Admiral Edels' assistant repeated. For as many in the room, his voice the only one heard. "Team Two surrounded half the building and cleared the rest, sir." He saluted, although no one returned the gesture.

"Where is team one?" Edels' graveled voice inquired.

"Most are on route back to the hotel, sir."

"What does that mean?" The Admiral's lack of patience shows.

"Half are accounted for. Two escorted Commander Atwood's daughter and complete family back to the boat, two are in between there, and the hotel, and," he took in a deep breath, "Rod and one other are M.I.A." swish, he exhaled out loud.

"Rod is tracking near the hotel," Pete said.

"How do you find him, son?" Edels asked.

"I have the tracking codes for everyone involved, sir," he watched Edels narrow his eyes towards his assistant. "I wished they moved faster." The room let out a nervous laugh.

Pete pressed a few keys before he reached over to fiddle with the black box in the center of the table. The screen on the wall split to show both the team whereabouts and the individuals he tracked.

"The other missing link is Ken Boci," he waited for someone to react. Both Atwood and Edels exchanged glances. "He went off-screen about two hours ago." Commander Atwood stood to a shuffling of chairs.

"Relax," a wave of his hand brought most back to sitting. "I need a sandwich, Pete?" he nodded towards the door.

"Yeah, I can use a bite, too." Once they moved away from the room, Pete asked, "Who knows about Boci besides the Admiral and us?"

"That is what I want to learn. Not one person seemed concerned he was off the radar." Atwood held open the cafeteria door. "I'd feel more comfortable if we knew his whereabouts."

Pete agreed. Both ordered plain turkey sandwiches from the deli. "Marjorie has been picked up, correct?" Atwood nodded. "What about Spencer?"

"Ah, Spencer," he laughed. "Spencer had video evidence Marjorie coerced, his words, him into this mess, and, you are going to love this one, he had been doing his own back investigation to obtain proof." Pete didn't speak. "So, Marjorie is in a holding cell in New York while Spencer walks free."

"With a tail?"

"With a tail."

"Don, this is insane. How'd we get here?"

"One dumbass son-in-law combined with a few greedy bastards, and, well, your family is wrong place…"

"Coincidence? Naw, remember this is all my sister's fault."

Zack could hear the grunts behind him coming from Sam and Celia. The hallway grew longer as the injured became weaker, transporting all a more demanding task. Rich not talking was his biggest worry. He brought his arm into position. Rich's pulse was weak yet present. He caught Ev watching him.
"I've been checking too," she said. Her voice is breathy. "And I still need a damn cigarette!"
"You are doing great, Ev," Zack said.
"No, I am not," she huffed. "How did you find us? Maxi said, you couldn't take time off from work."
"Did she now. Well, now's not the time for either story, and I promise they are both good ones."
Ev hiked up her husband's body. "Will you actually be able to tell the whole tale?"
"How about if I promise you once we are out of here sitting poolside, you and I will have a talk." Zack couldn't see Ev nod or the waterworks going down her cheeks. "I'll take that as a yes," he continued.

Maximum Trouble

At the juncture of the two hallways, Zack stopped. The trail of ketchup Celia had placed earlier led to the closest exit. In the opposite direction, a long walk back to the beach. Celia and Sam had Maxi's lifeless body leaning between them as all three rested against the wall. The pillowcase filled with supplies dragged behind Ric.

The weighted breath as the only sound.

The intelligent move would be to leave them all here and assess the area. He brought his attention to Maxi, her closed eyes, and slumped body against the cement wall. She had scraped up and down her body, along with a bruise on her cheek. Sam sported bruises across his face, arms, and from what Zack could see, his mid-section.

Ric squatted off to the side, his eyes bouncing between his mother and grandparents. He looked up at Zack. "Should we do something?"

"Yeah," Zack said, "we should" He took out his phone. No responses. "move back into the supply room down the hallway. From there, we can get a plan together and treat the wounded."

"Are you a doctor too?" Sam asked. "Because if you are—"

"I am not a doctor, but I have had first aid training—"

"This goes beyond first aid—"

"Shush, Sam. Let the man do his job."

Zack motioned to Ev to lift Rich. They half carried, half dragged him back into the supply room to sit him up in the far corner. Sam and Celia moved Maxi into the same area. Zack reached over to check her pulse. A weak beat stirred against his fingers. He took one of the water bottles out of the pillowcase, spilled the contents on a clean towel, and wiped her face. "Ric, are there any t-shirts or clothing on the shelves?" He waited.

"Nope. Just these," he held up a white maid's uniform. Zack motioned for Ric to bring it over.

"Ev and Celia," he changed positions, "would you two change their clothes?"

"Why?"

"So, they don't stink," Zack said. "Please, Ev." She walked around him towards Ric's voice. "Hang in there. I will be right back." He was out of the room before anyone could ask questions. Zack proceeded with caution as he kept his body in the shadows.

The closet exit leads outside in between two hotels. The foliage dividing the properties appeared dense. The concrete sidewalk led to the now covered in pink cement pieces beach or in the opposite direction, the main hotel lobby.

He went back inside. Either way would

Maximum Trouble

present challenges, yet the closest moved them away from danger faster.

Harmony and Mayala watched the front of the Seaview from inside the arranged seagrass that formed a perfect blind. More than once, the man in the tuxedo looked in their direction. And more than once, Mayala focused her gun on his heart.

"Not yet," Harmony's voice came above a whisper. "I want them all to meet their maker together.

"That may not be possible," Mayala fidgeted. The grass waved in front. "Who is missing now?" From their vantage, the man in the tuxedo walked in a circle. "Those behind him are not our friends—"

"Our cousins—"

"They are not from our island." Mayala pointed at the wrecked car out front. "That is Talin's car, no?" Harmony confirmed with a nod. "So, if Talin is dead—"

Maximum Trouble

"Talin is not dead," Harmony said. She shifted to face Mayala. "Talin is alive. He is here." Harmony's eyes grew black. "He is close."

Mayala nodded yet did not speak. More boys from the island clustered near the car. Some disappeared out of view on the opposite side. Most stayed clear of the man in the tuxedo. They watch as most left the Seaview, crossing the street to the mall.

In the brush behind, the two soldiers trained their rifles on the bodyguards. *I have a clear shot at the one on the left,* one signed. The other pointed at the guard on the right. *We need to take the leader alive, if possible.* The silent conversation continued while watching the two women huddled down below.

A third party, a single man, watched the interaction from behind a concrete pillar, upon the hotel driveway. He brought a small pair of binoculars up to his eyes. In his lens, the man in the tuxedo's glare. Neither moved.

Rod pocketed the glasses, turned to walk back to the other side of the mall. He had seen enough.

Ken Boci exited the lobby of the Seaview. He walked over to the man in the tuxedo, said a few words, and walked in the direct path of Harmony and Mayala. Both women stiffened with his approach.

Boci turned down the concrete path, disappearing around the corner. "He is dressed like Talin," Mayala said.
"He is the one who poisoned my Talin."
"We should kill him," Harmony's hand lowered Mayala's rifle before she could shoot. "All good things in all good time."
"You show great patience," Mayala sighed out.
"Patience? Not really. The opportunity will show itself, Mayala. I am waiting to see Talin's ugly face. I want him to watch me kill the devil inside him." Harmony's face, hands, and arms turned bright red. Mayala watched as she rubbed the pistol on her side.
She wondered what else Talin had done to bring such pain.

Maximum Trouble

On the screen, Team One arrived at the beach in the process of entering the far side of the Seaview. Team Two was in place on the opposite side of the mall. Zack and Rich's dot appeared in the same position on the screen.

"Team Two reported six young men dressed in the black t-shirts and shorts we observed earlier, have surrendered on the out of view part of the mall." Pete made a note on the legal pad in front of him. "Half of Team Two are escorting the group back on the party bus to the drop off point."

"Will we be taking care of discipline?"

"Believe it or not, the Dutch want to handle the situation with their citizens." Both men scoffed at the news.

"Figures." Pete clicked a few keys. "It appears they have taken back the rest of the island, on both sides of where we now have activity." Pete continued to click the keys. "Does this mean Team One will be meeting up with Brady and company soon?"

"I sure hope so. Pete, send Zack a message they are on their way."

Maximum Trouble

With both Rich and Maxi balanced, the rest of the party moved at a slog's pace towards the sunlight. Dust floated in and out of their destination as coughs and huffs filled the silence. Footsteps and non-English speakers danced in the distance.

Maxi remained in the semi-consciousness condition under the watchful eyes of her mother and son. Rich floated in and out, fully aware, looking for the plan, to mumbling his foot hurt. The rest struggled with the burden to carry. Zack's phone continued to vibrate. Instead of answering, he reached with his free hand to stop the notices.

There wasn't time. He had heard another explosion. The foundation vibrated in response. Cracks along the walls told him the building was losing its stability.

"Fancy meeting you here," Ken Boci took away half the sunlight in the exit. One of the giants from the lobby appeared to block the rest. The giant pointed an automatic assault rifle at

Zack. "Your gun, Mr. Brady," Boci slapped the giant in the shoulder. "Do you know how long I have waited for this," Boci rubbed his hands together. "What luck! We get bonuses for the man in the front!"

"Bonuses?" Zack threw his sidearm a few feet in front. It clanked on the cement. He stepped forward to block the rest of the group, stood with arms crossed, and waited.

"Zack, Zack, Zack, you are smarter than this." Zack's face went blank. "Really, man? Didn't you have a clue? They told me you were sharp. My wife especially thought you were a smarty pants. Oh boy, did I blow this one," laughter echoed then stopped. "Doesn't matter. Really it doesn't." Boci moved closer. "Oh, hey, you picked up a couple more. Great. Great." He reached in the direction of Maxi at the same moment Zack moved in front. "Is she?"

"No!" both Ev and Ric screamed.

"Good. Good. See all of you, well except you," he pointed at Zack, "are worth buku bucks alive." His hand waved about the space. "You, we have to kill to get paid. But that's okay. You understand this game, right, Zack? I mean, come on, you get it. After all, you played many times." Zack did not move. His stance was statuesque. "It doesn't matter if you do. Why Zack? Huh, do you know why?"

Boci let out a howl. "Because, Zack buddy, you are a royal pain in my ass," again, the laughter boomed.

Zack concentrated his scrutiny on Boci's moves, not his theatrics. The other man stayed put in the doorway. He stood at attention, yet anytime Boci moved, the giant followed with his eyes. Behind him, the occasional cough or sniffle, yet no words. Boci kicked his gun further away. He walked up in front of Zack, so close the horseradish on his breath loitered between them. The punch to the abdomen came swift and hard. Zack hunched over, releasing a grunt on contact.

"That is for being rude to my wife," Boci said through gritted teeth, he brought a second connection to Zack's chin, "That is for screwing up my plan and having a second connection to headquarters," he brought his fist back for a final strike, "And this—"

Harmony pointed towards Ken Boci, disappearing around the corner. "That is the killer of Phillippe," she said to Mayala. With a nod, Mayala moved through the brush to follow, gun ready for revenge. Harmony brought her attention back to Talin. The man in the tuxedo had vanished from view.
Talin stood tall in front of the hotel. His presence tugged at Harmony's heart for standing here is the love of her life, father of her only child. Her heart turned cold as she raised her gun, only to lower it back down.

Harmony moved out of the brush, now visible to her husband, if he should turn away from the mayhem. With light footsteps, she made her way towards him, dropping her weapons as she went.

The remaining soldier moved closer to her yet stayed in the shadows. His gun in hand, he was prepared to do what she might not be able.

"Talin," Harmony called out. He turned at his name. At first wide-eyed, his lips curved into a slow smile.

"My Harmony," his only words. She watched him move towards her, the bruise on her cheek aching. "My Harmony," he repeated, now only a few feet away. In her imagination, she saw Moony standing next to him, gun in hand. Her sweet Moony, dressed in black. Her sweet Moony.

Talin spread his arms to embrace her. She reached behind to bring the knife up. It connected within his stomach. A shriek let out from his lips. Talin, swift with the backhand, reconnected to the same bruise he put on Harmony's face earlier.

"You are the devil," he shouted. Talin raised his hand for another blow, blood splatter on the concrete, the wall, his cowering wife. A single gunshot. Harmony waited for the fire to rip through her. Talin's body fell by her side.

"Are you okay?" She heard a male voice yet did not move. A buzz sound came next. "Yes, sir. If I didn't shoot, he would have killed the mother." Harmony met the eye of one of the eight soldiers, dressed in full camouflage.

"Hang on, sir, are you alright?" She nodded. He helped her around her husband's body. She glanced back to see a single bullet hole in his forehead. "He started out decent," she told

the soldier, "He started out really good."
"They all do," the soldier said. "They all do."

Maximum Trouble

"**W**hat was that?" Ken Boci jumped in the direction of the gunshot. The guard stuck his head out to listen, came back in, and motioned with his shoulders. In perfect Russian, Boci yelled, "Well, freakin' find out," as the guard turned to leave, Ken called him back, adding in English, "no wait. Screw it. It doesn't matter. We have a task at hand here."

He brought his attention back inside. Zack Brady had regained his footing. Although not as sizeable as Ken or his guard, his presence took the rest out of view. Boci's face turned a dark shade of red. His handgun whirled into view. The bullet released quick.

Zack grabbed onto his right knee as he clasped to the ground. "I don't like you," Ken said. His voice calm and level. He brought his gun back into firing position. "You are a spoiled snot-nosed punk who made my wife's life hell, which made my life hell. That made me angry."

The rest jumped as a second bullet splattered blood from Zack's body. A high-pitched scream followed. Ken raised his gun again, this time in the direction of Maxi's slumped body. "You make him happy. You should—"

A voluptuous woman in a bright flowered dress appeared in the foliage. With her position, she could see right into the door. The team leader noted that one of his men followed about ten feet behind. As the woman came further in view, her rifle glittered in the sunlight.

"What the hell?" the team leader said into his two-way.

Through static, he could make out, "I told you I wasn't making this up. She's on our side."

"We are close. Now get her out of there." He watched his guy nod, then move to tap the woman on the shoulder. She brought her arm around to meet his helmet, yet the force knocked the soldier down. The ruckus had the guard outside the door, gun drawn.

With the moves of a dancer, Mayala brought her pistol into view. A single shot sent the guard stumbling back into the doorway. She turned towards the soldier, ready to fire another. He held his hands up high. "Jesus, lady," he said, "I'm on your side."

Mayala made the sign of the cross. "Do not use his name that way." She turned her attention back to the man in the Hawaiian shirt. Gunfire reverberated from within. Manic laughter followed, floating over screams.

Mayala jumped out of the bushes like a trained soldier brought her firearm to a level position. Her finger compressed the trigger, the man, in the middle of a laughing fit, fell to the ground.

Ken Boci's body clasped head first to the ground. A small pool of blood formed around his head. Sam moved to block Ric's view.

For a brief minute, no one moved. She mumbled a prayer before turning back at the soldier, who got back on his feet. He stood, mouth agape. "Lady, what the heck?"

Mayala put her gun on the ground. She held her hands in front. "I'm not going to arrest you," he said as he pushed passed.

"He killed my son," Mayala stated. "He might not have pulled the trigger, yet he killed my son." Her legs gave out, her body moved to a sitting position on the ground. She watched the others arrive, garbles of prayers floating from her lips.

The soldier took her hand in his, "We understand. We are here to help." Mayala put her head on his shoulder. His uniform became heavy with her tears.

A second soldier dressed in camouflage rushed by her, over to Zack's side. In his two-way, he yelled, "Medic stat!" He brought a cloth out of his front pocket, stuffed it in

Zack's stomach, then pressed down hard. "How the hell did you miss?" he shouted in Mayala's direction.

"She didn't," Ev, who now kneeled next to him, said. "That asshole next to him did this."

Celia took the pillowcase from Ric. She handed Ev clean towels along with gauze and alcohol. The soldier grabbed at each item, a quiet thank you with each addition.

Mayala sat on the stairs. She watched. Her lips moved in silent prayers.

More people arrived along with portable stretchers and first aid kits. The hallway became dense with bodies moving. Two assisted Ev and Rich out of the building. A red sun hovered above the turquoise ocean. Maxi followed in a soldier's arms, Ric by his side.

A man wearing a red cross on his helmet examined Rich's foot, shouted something to a group a short distance away, and pointed towards the mall. Within a minute, the party bus pulled up in the hotel drive.

"Don't tell Brady I carried his gal," the soldier said to Ric. He helped both board. "Mam, we need to get your husband and daughter to a hospital—"

"What about the others?" Celia and Sam spoke with another soldier a few feet away. He pointed towards the bus.

"They are going on the bus too." Ev nodded.

Maximum Trouble

"Where's Zack?"

"Commander Brady is in good hands—"

"That's not what I asked," Ev started to walk back towards the side entrance. "He's family." She pushed passed the group of soldiers smoking on the side. Mayala still sat in the doorway. In front of her lay Ken Boci's body.

"Where's—"

"They took him away."

"What does that mean, they took him away?" Mayala pointed in the opposite direction. Ev started to move when an arm pulled her back. Mayala held on tight. She shook her head.

"Damn it," Ev brushed a tear away. "I need a god-damn cigarette."

Commander Atwood sat at his desk, phone in hand, scribbling on a legal pad. Pete, from his spot at the temporary table, watched his computer screen. He half-listened to the "ah ha's," "you don't say," and his favorite, "I hope you got a picture of that one."

Pete waited until Atwood finished writing notes before he asked, "Good news, sir?"

"Yes and no." He looked down at his legal pad. "My daughter and her family are on the aircraft carrier. They are safe for now. My dipshit son-in-law informed me although he still holds the launch codes, they are in a safe place, so I shouldn't worry."

Pete coughed to hide a laugh. Atwood continued, "The rebel's island contact, some guy named Talin, along with Ken Boci, are both dead. Killed by natives." Pete watched the commander. "Actually, one by his wife and the other a cousin."

"Never mess with a pissed off woman," Pete said.

"The man in the tuxedo who the natives say is the one in charge, is missing. Rod hasn't reported in either."

He turned the page. "And my family?"

"Your father and sister are at a makeshift hospital along with the other members of their party. Zack Brady..." The commander looked directly at Pete, "is in critical condition with two gunshot wounds, knee, and stomach."

"Jesus." Pete sat back in the chair and stared at the wall. "Is he going to make it?"

"They are attempting to fly him to the ship's infirmary."

Pete clicked a few buttons on the computer. "Please keep me in the loop."

Rod walked across the empty island in the direction of the airport. Several Humvees passed his path as more troops from the States traveled between the airport and hotel row. His instructions appeared simple; rendezvous at the abandoned Marquee Resort with any operatives who remain.

With his presence in plain sight, Rod opted for the beach route. He crossed at La Cabana to walk down to the ocean's edge on the wooden planks that ran from the road to the high tide mark. The soft, warm breeze gave a sense of calm from the absence of people along with the popular bathing spot.

Rod sped up his stride. He took the same path into the resort as Maxi had only days prior. Like Maxi, his first thought of the water cooler guided his route. Rod filled a paper cup and moved into the pool area, now with a full view of any who may enter.

Maximum Trouble

He took a long sip, sat back, and waited. His contract was almost complete.

Ev sat on the bench outside of Oduber Hospital. She took a long inhale of the burning tobacco between her fingers as she stared at the peeks of the Caribbean Sea between two waterfront buildings. A cool breeze along her right side indicated the front door had opened. Ric sat down next to her.
"Hey, kid," she took another long inhale.
"Hey Gram," Ric responded as he stared at the same view. "Some vacation, huh?"
"You got that right." He leaned over to rest his head on her shoulder. Ev put her arm around her grandson. "This will all be okay."
"How do you know this, Gram?" He turned his head up towards hers.
"Well, I don't, but look at what happened so far," Ric waited for her to continue. Ev reached over towards the planter near the end of the bench. She snuffed the end of her cigarette out and left it with the others. A sign above the pile reads the container's function is

a planter, not an ashtray.
"What do you mean?"
Ev forced out a long exhale of smoke in the opposite direction of her grandson. "They fixed Papa's foot. That is good news." Ric mumbled agreement. "And your mom should be able to travel home soon, too."
His hand snaked around her waist. Ev moved her head to the side to see her grandson's closed eyes. His breath was keeping beat with his heart. She brushed his hair off of his forehead as a commercial plane took off over the ridge.

L.M. Pampuro

Pete walked back towards the conference room. Once outside, he found both Admiral Edels and Commander Atwood in deep conversation. "We should be ready to go in about a half-hour." He moved out of view, cellphone in hand. In perfect Russian, Pete spoke, "Cherez chas my vysadimsya. Prigotov'sya (We will be landing in an hour. Be prepared)." He walked back around the two men to enter the room.

Two men sat poolside as the sun dropped onto the horizon line. Bright shades of red, orange, blue, and purple filled the sky. Glasses filled with clear liquid sat within reach of both along with bags of potato chips, vending machine cookies, and an empty pizza box. Used napkins blew away in the salted wind.

Neither rose to retrieve the waste.

Rod's cellphone vibrated in his pocket. "Aren't you going to answer?" the man next to him asked. Now stripped down to red Bermuda

shorts and a white undershirt, his stature dwindled with his lost attire.
"No need." In his sightline, a black tuxedo is out of place, under an umbrella. "Is that a signal of some sort?"
The other man nodded no. "Signal," he laughed. "For what? You know the plan as well as I."
Rod went back to a slow nod. "They should be here at dark." Little sparkles of white began to stretch across the sky along with a sliver of a moon. "Here's to Cuba," he said as he lifted his glass.
"I will only drink to Putin," the other responded.
"Okay, I drink to Putin and those who transfer the coin." They clinked glasses. The liquid burned against their throats. "You will not betray me?"
The smaller man expresses amusement. "As you would not betray me," he answered, adding, "Since neither of us possesses the codes…"
They observed each other with neutral expressions. Both in their own silence.

Commander Atwood nodded in Pete's direction as they entered. "Are we ready to get rid of the pollution?" he asked.

"Yes, sir," Pete answered with a salute. He leaned over his computer and typed in *Directive 49, 86, 13.*

The response came back within minutes. *10-100.* "Both?" Commander Atwood asked.

"Both," Peter replied.

Maximum Trouble

The waiting room's yellow walls and bright paintings of the sun setting over various Naval ships wore thin on Maxi's nerves. She watched the clock in the corner move slightly passed the ten. She arrived at eight, like every other day the previous two weeks. She checked in, and like every morning prior, she was told due to HIPPA laws, they couldn't let her see Zack without a family member present.

First, Zack's stepdaughter, Lilly, walked her in. The two didn't talk much. Both sat watching Zack breath on the machines. Lilly moved in and out of the room quite a bit, always with a tilt of the head towards her cellphone. She took her father's situation in stride as she acted more like an obligatory visitor than his relative.

When Lilly left, Gracie arrived. Zack's daughter took over where her sister left off. She demanded updates and hounded every nurse who entered. She checked his diet, although he took food intravenous, yet she complained he didn't get enough of specific vitamins.

Lilly brought Maxi in every day. Gracie made her wait until she got a full report from both Zack's doctor and any attending nurse within her view. Maxi wondered if Gracie understood the reports or nodded and "ah ha'd" at the appropriate time.

"I learned a lot about medicine working on the soap," she had informed Maxi. "We need to keep an eye on these folks." Maxi would nod yet not speak. After a few days of this routine, Gracie inquired why Maxi wasn't on the permanent guest list.

"Your father is in Intensive Care. Visits are allowed from immediate family only. There are—"

"—HIPPA laws. Blah blah, I get it," she yelled at the nurse. "This is my dad's significant other. She needs to see him." Maxi started to correct Gracie then thought the better of it. Any bloke in a bar who can help her. "You should call your brother," Gracie suggested. "I bet he could get you passed these," she paused for effect, "people."

Maxi made the call. Gracie went back to the city. Maxi still sat in the lobby waiting with the U.S.S. Ronald Regan, the U.S.S. Alaska, the U.S.S. Cole, and others surrounding her on the wall. Beautiful sunsets with large, gray Navy boats in the center.

"Commander Atwood," Maxi jumped out of her daze as her brother's boss entered the room.

"Oh," he hesitated before addressing her by her proper name, "Mary Alexis, yes, how are you feeling?"

"Better," she said. "Much better, thanks." The two stood in silence before Maxi asked, "Are you here to see Zack?" The commander nodded. "Tell him I said hi, I guess."

"Tell him yourself."

"I would love to, but Gracie, Zack's daughter, put me on the list when she was here and then that nurse," she pointed at the receptionist, "said I couldn't go in without a relative, so I put in a call to Pete, but you know how busy he is, so I sit out here waiting for someone to let me in to sit with Zack because I am the reason—" Maxi explained her predicament in one long breath before she brought her hands up to her eyes. She rubbed away her wet frustrations.

"Mary Alexis," the commander put his arm around her shoulder, "who told you that?" She opened her mouth to speak, yet with a wave, silenced. "You are not, in any way, shape or form, the reason for any of this," his voice reassured. "You were in the wrong place at the wrong time. That's all. It happens."

She took a long breath. When she exhaled, her body shook. "Thank you," she said, her voice above a whisper as she added, "Can you tell my mother that?"

Commander Atwood's laugh caught the attention of those in the room. "Come on," he steered her towards the receptionist, "Let's get you in to see your man.

It took Commander Atwood one conversation along with a three-minute phone call to move Maxi from the waiting room to Zack's. Another ten minutes, he moved her name to the permitted visitor's list and gave her access to his medical diagnosis.

"The caveat to all this is you need to give me daily updates on Agent Brady's condition."

The nurses stood in the hallway to watch the man and woman in intensive care. The woman held his hand and spoke in a quiet voice. She smiled when she faced him, yet when she turned away, one could watch her free hand wipe her eyes. If she looked in their direction, they gave a small smile and sometimes waved.

It had been over a week since Maxi's mother found Zack. To say Ev was persistent in the process would be an understatement. She hounded Pete's boss while she called every hospital, first on the island, then in the D.C.

area. Once found, Ev did the unthinkable. She got him moved to Hartford Hospital.

Because of her mom, Maxi sat holding Zack's hand, every day, for the last month.

The machines became her symphony, the beep of his heart her lifeline. The lights made patterns on the drab gray walls, while the soft lights brought on a comfort no one should need to feel.

Her parents, Ric, Pete, and Zack's two daughters, took turns to give Maxi a break. They sent her on walks around the hospital, food runs, and other errands, which often brought her to the meditation room. A place she sat and cried without judgment of others or herself.

The nurses thought she was his loyal wife. They addressed her as Mrs. Brady. She'd open her mouth to correct yet usually just forced a small smile in their direction.

"Now you listen to me, Zack Brady," Maxi squeezed his hand as she spoke, "you need to wake up and smell the damn roses because I will not have you this way because of me. Wait – I take that back, I will not have you this way, period. You and I...," she stopped for a moment. To those passing by, she appeared pensive, yet like a duck, she paddled madness under the surface.

"You and I cannot keep saving each other, although this time it wasn't me, it was Mayala.

Hold on, you don't know her, do you? She is this really fabulous island person who shot that horse's ass who shot you. You'll meet her," Maxi waved off the remark with her opposite hand. "You'll love her."

The nurse came in to fidget with one of the tubes. Her movements were efficient. She replaced the bag of liquid connected to Zack's arm and checked the wiring on the heart machine in two swift motions.

"How are you doing today, Miss?" she spoke as she stepped about the room, checking connections, rotating equipment.

"I'm okay, you?"

She reached over to take Maxi's free hand in hers. "This too shall pass," she said. She squeezed Maxi's hand and turned to leave.

"What was that?" Maxi stared at her, and Zack's joined hands.

"What?" the nurse jumped back by her side. They both watched as Zack's fingers spasmed. "I'll be damned," the nurse said. "Rub your fingers along his. I will be right back." She hurried out of the room.

Maxi concentrated on the sensation of her fingers motion against Zack's jerks. She began to speak to him, "I can feel you move, Zack, I can feel you. Please let me know if you can hear me. Please?" His fingers stopped. "Don't leave me now, Zack, don't leave me..."

Maximum Trouble

The doctor rushed by Maxi. He forced their connection to end as the nurse hurried her out of the room. "What is happening?" Maxi asked. She followed the nurse back into the waiting room.

"Sit tight," the nurse said as she turned to dash back in the direction they just vacated.

"Keep talking to him," the doctor instructed as he wrote something on Zack's chart. He handed the information back to the nurse. "And make certain you check on him more frequently," he scolded. The nurse stuck her tongue out when the doctor turned back to Zack.

This brought a smile to Maxi's face. The nurse scrunched her nose. Maxi started to giggle.

"She's making faces at me, isn't she?" The nurse shook her head no. Maxi fell into full-blown laughter. "Very mature, Irma," he said as he exited the room.

She held both her hands tight to Zack's. She stroked his skin with both her thumbs. His lips bent into a slight smile, eyes closed, breath steady. "Come on, Zack, wake up," she encouraged. "Just wake up... for me."
The yawn caught her off guard. She didn't move as his eyes fought to open. Maxi watched as, like a butterfly emerging from a cocoon, Zack Brady returned to the living. He rotated his head around the room to focus on his hands. His eyes followed the connection

along her arm, up her neck, to her face.
His lips bent further up.
"Hello," his voice raspy yet clear. "Hello, my beautiful."

Maximum Trouble

L.M. Pampuro

Thank you's

I'll start with the obvious; thanks to my family for their love and support. Although I find the family stories interesting, none appear in this book.

Thanks to my beta-readers: Robert Calegari, Evelyn Pampuro, Eileen Waldman, Terri Meigs, and Hollie Rose. Your feedback was perfect and appreciated!

Thanks to the folks of CoLoNY for peace, love, and understanding. You ladies rock!

Thanks to The Harmony Café for the best breakfast sandwiches and homemade Chai tea. The creative vibe comes alive in your place.

My ongoing thanks and appreciation to Chris Archer, Kay Janney, Jamie Cat Callan, and Jim Parise.

And finally, thank you to my readers and supporters. Writing is good for my head yet for your ongoing outpouring of good energy, I am eternally grateful

Also, by L.M. Pampuro,

Dancing With Faith

Maximum Mayhem (Zack & Maxi's 1ˢᵗ adventure)

The Perfect Pitch

Passenger: the only game in town

Uncle Neddy's Funeral

Maximum Trouble

Harlot's grace

Harlot's fire

Visit her at Pampuro.com

Maximum Trouble